"You can take care of yourself, right? Never need any help."

"I wouldn't say that." Frankie opened her door and got out.

Hank swore and, throwing the pickup into Park, got out and went after her. "Frankie, wait."

She stopped and turned back to him.

"I don't know what your story is, but I do know this," he said. "You have closed yourself off for some reason. I recognize the signs because I've done it for the past three years. In your case, I suspect some man's to blame, the one who keeps calling. One question. Is he dangerous?"

She started to step away, but he grabbed her arm and pulled her back around to face him again.

"I'm fine. There is nothing to worry about."

He shook his head but let go of her arm. "You are one stubborn woman."

He couldn't help but smile because there was a strength and independence in her that he admired.

He'd never known a woman quite like her...

IRON WILL

New York Times Bestselling Author

B.J. DANIELS

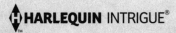

This one is for Paula Morrison, who believes like I do that if one schlep bag is a great idea, then let's make a dozen. Thanks for making Quilting by the Border quilt club so fun.

ISBN-13: 978-1-335-64099-4

Iron Will

Copyright © 2019 by Barbara Heinlein

PLEASE RECYCLE
THIS PRODUCT IS RECYCLABLE

Recycling programs
for this product may
not exist in your area.

This edition published by arrangement with Harlequin Books S.A.

For questions and comments about the quality of this book, please contact us at CustomerService@Harlequin.com.

® and TM are trademarks of Harlequin Enterprises Limited or its corporate affiliates. Trademarks indicated with ® are registered in the United States Patent and Trademark Office, the Canadian Intellectual Property Office and in other countries.

Printed in U.S.A.

HARLEQUIN®
www.Harlequin.com

B.J. Daniels is a *New York Times* and *USA TODAY* bestselling author. She wrote her first book after a career as an award-winning newspaper journalist and author of thirty-seven published short stories. She lives in Montana with her husband, Parker, and three springer spaniels. When not writing, she quilts, boats and plays tennis. Contact her at bjdaniels.com, on Facebook or on Twitter, @bjdanielsauthor.

Books by B.J. Daniels

Visit the Author Profile page at Harlequin.com.

CAST OF CHARACTERS

Hank Savage—The cowboy doubts he'll ever get over the death of his first love. But now he's back at Cardwell Ranch, determined to prove she was murdered. And he didn't come alone.

Francesca "Frankie" Brewster—The PI was hesitant to take the case. But she had her own reasons for wanting to leave town right now.

Naomi Hill—She wanted the fantasy—marriage, a home, a husband with a good job and the kids—and she'd do almost anything to get it. Even die.

Randall "Butch" Clark—He was more than Naomi's former boyfriend. He was her confidant, so he knew her secrets.

Tamara Baker—The bartender might have messed up a few too many times and now it was going to cost her.

Darrel Sanders—All he was doing was trying to make a living and keep from getting killed.

Carrie White—Her best friend seemed to have everything that Naomi had ever wanted.

Marshal Hud Savage—He'd dreamed of reconciling with his son. Now Hank was back, so why was he suspicious?

Dana Cardwell Savage—The ranchwoman wanted only two things. For her son to come home and for him to put Naomi and the past behind him. Was she going to get more than she'd hoped for?

Chapter One

Hank Savage squinted into the sun glaring off the dirty windshield of his pickup as his family ranch came into view. He slowed the truck to a stop, resting one sun-browned arm over the top of the steering wheel as he took in the Cardwell Ranch.

The ranch with all its log-and-stone structures didn't appear to have changed in the least. Nor had the two-story house where he'd grown up. Memories flooded him of hours spent on the back of a horse, of building forts in the woods around the creek, of the family sitting around the large table in the kitchen in the mornings, the sun pouring in, the sound of laughter. He saw and felt everything he'd given up, everything he'd run from, everything he'd lost.

"Been a while?" asked the sultry, dark-haired woman in the passenger seat.

He nodded despite the lump in his throat,

shoved back his Stetson and wondered what the hell he was doing back here. This was a bad idea, probably his worst ever.

"Having second thoughts?" He'd warned her about his big family, but she'd said she could handle it. He wasn't all that sure even he could handle it. He prided himself on being fearless about most things. Give him a bull that hadn't been ridden and he wouldn't hesitate to climb right on. Same with his job as a lineman. He'd faced gale winds hanging from a pole to get the power back on, braved getting fried more times than he liked to remember.

But coming back here, facing the past? He'd never been more afraid. He knew it was just a matter of time before he saw Naomi—just as he had in his dreams, in his nightmares. She was here, right where he'd left her, waiting for him as she had been for three long years. Waiting for him to come back and make things right.

He looked over at Frankie. "You sure about this?"

She sat up straighter to gaze at the ranch and him, took a breath and let it out. "I am if you are. After all, this was your idea."

Like she had to remind him. "Then I suggest you slide over here." He patted the seat between them and she moved over, cuddling against him as he put his free arm around her. She felt small and fragile, certainly not ready for what he suspected they would be facing. For a moment, he almost changed his mind. It wasn't too late. He didn't have the right to involve her.

"It's going to be okay," she said and nuzzled his neck where his dark hair curled at his collar. "Trust me."

He pulled her closer and let his foot up off the brake. The pickup began to roll toward the ranch. It wasn't that he didn't trust Frankie. He just knew that it was only a matter of time before Naomi came to him pleading with him to do what he should have done three years ago. He felt a shiver even though the summer day was unseasonably warm.

I'm here.

Chapter Two

"Looking out that window isn't going to make him show up any sooner," Marshal Hud Savage said to his wife.

"I can't help being excited. It's been three years." Dana Cardwell Savage knew she didn't need to tell him how long it had been. Hud had missed his oldest son as much or more than she had. But finally Hank was coming home—and bringing someone with him. "Do you think it's because he's met someone that he's coming back?"

Hud put a large hand on her shoulder. "Let's not jump to any conclusions, okay? We won't know anything until he gets here. I just don't want to see you get your hopes up."

Her hopes were already up, so there was no mitigating that. Family had always been the most important thing to her. Having her sons all fly the nest had been heartbreak, especially Hank, especially under the circumstances.

She told herself not to think about that. Nothing was going to spoil this day. Her oldest son was coming home after all this time. That had to be good news. And he was bringing someone. She hoped that meant Hank was moving on from Naomi.

"Is that his pickup?" she cried as a black truck came into view. She felt goose bumps pop up on her arms. "I think that's him."

"Try not to cry and make a fuss," her husband said even as tears blurred her eyes. "Let them at least get into the yard," he said as she rushed to the front door and threw it open. "Why do I bother?" he mumbled behind her.

FRANKIE KNEW THE sixty-two-year-old woman who rushed out on the porch had to be Dana Cardwell Savage. Hank had told her about his family. She thought about the softness that came into his voice when he talked about his mother. She'd heard about Dana's strength and determination, but she could also see it in the way she stood hugging herself in her excitement and her curiosity.

Hank had warned her that him bringing home a woman would cause a stir. Frankie could see his mother peering inside the pickup, trying to imagine what woman had stolen her son's heart. She felt a small stab of guilt but quickly pushed it away as a man appeared behind Dana.

Marshal Hud Savage. She'd also heard a lot about him. When Hank had mentioned his dad, she'd seen the change not just in his tone, but his entire body. The trouble between the two ran deep. While Dana was excited, holding nothing back, Frankie could see that Hud was reserved. He had to worry that this wouldn't be a happy homecoming considering the way he'd left things with his oldest son.

Hank's arm tensed around her as he parked and cut the engine. She had the feeling that he didn't want to let her go. He finally eased his hold on her, then gave her a gentle squeeze. "We can do this, right? Ready?"

"As I will ever be," she said, and he opened his door. The moment he did, Dana rushed down the steps to throw her arms around her son. Tears streamed down her face unchecked. She hugged him, closing her eyes, breathing him in as if she'd thought she might never see him again.

Frankie felt her love for Hank at heart level. She slowly slid under the steering wheel and stepped down. Hud, she noticed, had descended the stairs, but stopped at the bottom, waiting, unsure of the reception he was going to get. Feeling for him, she walked around mother and son to address him.

"Hi, I'm Frankie. Francesca, but everyone calls me Frankie." She held out her hand, and the marshal accepted it in his large one as his gaze took her measure. She took his as well. Hud Savage was scared that this visit wasn't an olive branch. Scared that his son was still too angry with him. Probably more scared that he was going to let down his wife by spoiling this reunion.

"It's nice to meet you," the marshal said, his voice rough with what she suspected was emotion. A lot was riding on what would happen during this visit, she thought, and Hud didn't know the half of it.

"Frankie," Hank said behind her. His voice broke. "I want you to meet my mom, Dana."

She turned and came face-to-face with the ranch woman. Dana had been a beauty in her day; anyone could see that. But even in her sixties, she was still very attractive with her salt-and-pepper dark hair and soft, gentle features. She was also a force to be reckoned with. Dana eyed her like a mama bear, one who was sizing her up for the position of daughter-in-law.

Whatever Dana saw and thought of her, the next thing Frankie knew, she was being crushed in the woman's arms. "It is so wonderful to meet you," Dana was saying tearfully.

Behind her, Frankie heard Hud say hello to his son.

"Dad," Hank said with little enthusiasm, and then Dana was ushering them all into the house, telling her son that she'd baked his favorite cookies and made his favorite meal.

Frankie felt herself swept up in all of it as she told herself this would work out—even against her better judgment.

"HANK SEEMS GOOD, doesn't he," Dana said later that night when the two of them were in bed. She'd told herself that things had gone well and that once Hank was home for a while, they would get even better. She hadn't been able to ignore the tension between her son and husband. It made her heart ache because she had no idea how to fix the problem.

"He seems fine." Hud didn't look up from the crime novel he was reading.

"Frankie is pretty, isn't she."

"Uh-huh."

"She's not what I expected. Not really Hank's type, don't you think?"

Hud glanced over at her. "It's been three years since we've seen him. We have no idea what his type is. He probably doesn't know either. He's still young. I thought Naomi wasn't his type." He went back to his book.

"He's thirty-three, not all that young if he wants to have a family," she said. "It's just that Frankie isn't anything like Naomi."

"Maybe that's the attraction."

She heard what he didn't say in his tone. *Maybe that's a blessing.* Hud had never thought Naomi was right for Hank. "I suppose it might be why he's attracted to her. I just never thought he'd get over Naomi."

Hud reached over and, putting down his book, turned out his bedside light. "Good night," he said pointedly.

She took the hint and switched off her own lamp as her husband rolled over, turning his back to her. Within minutes he would be sound asleep, snoring lightly, while she lay awake worrying. The worst part was that she couldn't put her finger on what made her anxious about Hank coming home now and bringing a young woman.

"He wants to move on, put Naomi and all that ugliness behind him, don't you think?" She glanced over at Hud's broad back, but knew he wasn't going to answer because he didn't have the answer any more than she did.

She was just glad that Hank was home

for however long he planned to stay and that he wasn't alone anymore. "As long as he's happy..." Hud began to snore softly. She sighed and closed her eyes, silently mouthing her usual nightly prayers that her family all be safe and happy, and thanking God for bringing Hank home.

"IT'S BEAUTIFUL HERE," Frankie said as she stood on the guest cabin deck overlooking the rest of the ranch in the starlight. The cabin was stuck back high against the mountain looking down on the ranch and the Gallatin River as it wound past. "I feel like I can see forever. Are those lights the town?" she asked as Hank joined her.

"Big Sky, Montana," he said with little enthusiasm.

She turned to him. "How do you think it went?"

He shook his head. "I'm just thankful that my mother listened to me and didn't have the whole family over tonight. But maybe it would have been less uncomfortable if they'd all been there. Tomorrow you'll meet my sister, Mary, and her fiancé, Chase."

"There's your uncle Jordan and aunt Stacy."

"And a bunch of my mother's cousins and their families," he said with a sigh.

She couldn't imagine having all that family. Her father had left when she was three. Her mother had married several times, but the marriages didn't last. Her mother had died in a car accident right after she'd graduated from high school, but they'd never been close. The only real family she'd ever felt she had was an uncle who'd become her mentor after college, but he was gone now too.

"You could just tell them the truth," she said quietly after a moment. She envied Hank his family, and felt lying to them was a mistake.

He shook his head. "This is difficult enough." He turned to go back inside. "You can have the first bedroom. I'll take the other one." With that, he went inside and closed the door.

Frankie stood on the deck, the summer night a fragrant blend of pine and water. There was just enough starlight that she caught glimpses of it shining off the surface of the river snaking through the canyon. Steep, rocky cliffs reflected the lights of the town, while the mountains rose up into the midnight-blue star-filled canopy.

She felt in awe of this ranch and his family. How could Hank have ever left it behind? But the answer seemed to be on the breeze as if everything about this place was inhabited by one woman. Naomi. She was what had brought Hank home. She was also why Frankie was here.

Chapter Three

Hank rose before the sun and made his way down the mountainside to the corral. He'd missed the smell of saddle leather and horse-flesh. He was breathing it in when he heard someone approaching from behind him.

He'd always been keenly aware of his environment. Growing up in Montana on a ranch, he'd learned at a young age to watch out for things that could hurt you—let alone kill you—in the wild. That instinct had only intensified in the years he'd been gone as if he felt a darkness trailing him, one that he could no longer ignore.

"You're up early," he said to his father without turning around as Hud came up behind him.

"I could say the same about you. I thought you and I should talk."

"Isn't that what we did at dinner last night?" Hank asked sarcastically. His father hadn't said ten words. Instead his mother had filled in the awkward silences.

"I'm glad you came back," Hud said.

He turned finally to look at his father. The sun glowed behind the mountain peaks to the east, rimming them with a bright orange glow. He studied his father in the dim light. They were now both about the same height, both with broad shoulders and slim hips. Both stubborn to a fault. Both never backing down from a fight. He stared at the marshal, still angry with him after all these years.

"I'm not staying long."

Hud nodded. "That's too bad. Your mother will be disappointed. So am I. Son—"

"There really isn't anything to talk about, is there? We said everything we had to say three years ago. What would be the point of rehashing it?"

"I stand by what I did."

Hank laughed. "I'd be shocked if you didn't." He shook his head. "It must be wonderful to know that you're always right."

"I'm not always right. I just do the best I can with the information and evidence I have."

"Well, you're wrong this time," he said and turned back to the horses. One of the mares had come up to have her muzzle rubbed. Behind him, he heard his father head back toward the house and felt some of the tension in his chest release even as he cursed under his breath.

DANA HAD INSISTED on making them breakfast. After a stack of silver-dollar-sized pancakes swimming in butter and huckleberry syrup, a slab of ham, two eggs over easy and a tall glass of orange juice, Frankie sat back smiling. She couldn't remember the last time she'd eaten so much or liked it more.

No matter what happened on this visit to the ranch, she planned to enjoy herself as much as was possible.

"I thought dinner was amazing," she told Dana. Hank's favorite meal turned out to be roast beef, mashed potatoes, carrots and peas and homemade rolls. "But this breakfast... It was so delicious. I never eat like this."

"I can tell by your figure," her host said, beaming. Clearly Dana equated food with love as she looked to her son to see if he'd enjoyed it. He'd cleaned his plate, which seemed to make her even happier. "So, what do you two have planned today?"

"I thought I'd show Frankie around Big Sky," Hank said.

"Well, it's certainly changed since you were here," his mother said. "I think you'll be surprised. Will you two be back for lunch? Your father still comes home every day at twelve."

"I think we'll get something in town, but thanks, Mom. Thanks for everything."

Tears filled her eyes and her voice broke when she spoke. "I'm just glad to have you home. Now, plan on being here for supper. Your dad's doing steaks on the grill and some of the family is stopping by. Not everyone. We don't want to overwhelm Frankie."

"I appreciate that," he said.

Frankie offered to help with the dishes, but Dana shooed them out, telling them to have a fun day.

Fun was the last thing on the agenda, she thought as she left with Hank.

HANK HAD BEEN restless all morning, but he'd known that he couldn't get away from the house without having one of his mother's breakfasts. The last thing he wanted to do was hurt her feelings. It would be bad enough when she learned the truth.

Pushing that thought away, he concentrated on his driving as he headed downriver. He'd grown up with the Gallatin River in his backyard. He hadn't thought much about it until Frankie was doing her research and asked him, "Did you know that the Gallatin River begins in the northwest corner of Yellowstone National Park to travel one hundred and twenty miles through the Gallatin Canyon past Big Sky to join the Jefferson and Madison Rivers to form the Missouri River?"

That she found this so fascinating had surprised him. "I did know that," he told her and found himself studying her with renewed interest. The river had been part of his playground, although he'd been taught to have a healthy respect for it because of the current, the deep holes and the slippery rocks.

Now as he drove along the edge of the Gallatin as it cut through the rocky cliffs of the canyon, he caught glimpses of the clear green water rushing over granite boulders on its way to the Gulf of Mexico and felt a shiver because he'd learned just how deadly it could be.

A few miles up the road, he slowed to turn onto a dirt road that wound through the tall pines. Dust rose behind the pickup. He put down his window and breathed in the familiar scents. They made his heart ache.

Ahead, he could see the cliffs over the top of the pines. He parked in the shade of the trees and sat for a moment, bracing himself.

"This is the place?" Frankie whispered, her gaze on the cliff that could be seen over the top of the pines.

He didn't answer as he climbed out. He heard her exit the pickup but she didn't follow him as he walked down through the thick pines toward the river, knowing he needed a few minutes alone.

An eerie silence filled the air. When he'd first gotten out of the truck, he'd heard a squirrel chatting in a nearby tree, a meadowlark calling from the tall grass, hoppers buzzing as they rose with each step.

But now that he was almost to the spot, there was no sound except the gentle lap of the water on the rocks. As he came out of the pines, he felt her—just as he always had. Naomi. It was as if her soul had been stranded here in this very spot where she'd died.

His knees went weak and he had to sit down on one of the large boulders along the shore. He put his head in his hands, unaware of time passing. Unaware of anything but his pain.

Like coming out of a daze, he lifted his head and looked across the river to the deep pool beneath the cliff. Sunlight glittered off the clear emerald surface. His heart in his throat, he lifted his gaze to the rock ledge high above the water. Lover's Leap. That was what it was called.

His gaze shifted to the trail from the bridge downriver. It was barely visible through the tall summer grass and the pines, but he knew that kids still traveled along it to the ledge over the water. The trick, though, was to jump out far enough. Otherwise…

A shaft of sun cut through the pine boughs that hung out over the water, nearly blinding him. He closed his eyes again as he felt Naomi pleading with him to find out the truth. He could feel her arguing that he knew her. He knew she was terrified of heights. She would never have gone up there. Especially alone. Especially at night. Why would she traverse the treacherous trail to get to the rock ledge to begin with—let alone jump?

It had made no sense.

Not unless she hadn't jumped to her death. Not unless she'd been pushed.

Hank opened his eyes and looked up through the shaft of sunlight to see a figure moving along the narrow trail toward the rock ledge high on the cliff. His throat went dry as shock ricocheted through him. He started to call to her even as he knew it was his mind playing tricks on him. It wasn't Naomi.

He opened his mouth, but no sound came out and he stared frozen in fear as he recognized the slim figure. Frankie. She'd walked downriver to the bridge and, after climbing up the trail, was now headed for the ledge.

HUD HEAVED HIMSELF into his office chair, angry at himself on more levels than he wanted to contemplate. He swore as he unlocked the bottom drawer of his desk and pulled out the file. That he'd kept it for three years in the locked drawer where he could look at it periodically was bad enough. That he was getting it out now and going over it as he'd done so many times over those years made it even worse.

He knew there was nothing new in the file. He could practically recite the report by heart. Nothing had changed. So why was he pulling it out now? What good would it do to go over it again? None.

But he kept thinking about Hank and his stubborn insistence that Naomi hadn't committed suicide. He didn't need a psychiatrist to tell him that suicide was the most perverse of deaths. Those left behind had to deal with the guilt and live with the questions that haunted them. Why hadn't they known? Why hadn't they helped? Why had she killed herself? Was it because of them? It was the why that he knew his son couldn't accept.

Why would a beautiful young woman like Naomi Hill kill herself? It made no sense.

Hud opened the file. Was it possible there was something he'd missed? He knew that wasn't the case and yet he began to go over it, remembering the call he'd gotten that morning from the fisherman who'd found her body in the rocks beneath Lover's Leap.

There had been little doubt about what had happened. Her blouse had caught on a rock on the ledge, leaving a scrap of it fluttering in the wind. The conclusion that she'd either accidentally fallen or jumped was later changed to suicide after more information had come in about Naomi's state of mind in the days before her death.

Add to that the coroner's report. Cause of death: skull crushed when victim struck the rocks below the cliff after either falling or jumping headfirst.

But his son Hank had never accepted it and had never forgiven his father for not investigating her death longer, more thoroughly. Hank had believed that Naomi hadn't fallen or jumped. He was determined that she'd been murdered.

Unfortunately, the evidence said otherwise, and Hud was a lawman who believed in facts—not conjecture or emotion. He still did and that was the problem, wasn't it?

Chapter Four

Hank felt dizzy and sick to his stomach as he watched Frankie make her way out to the edge of the cliff along the narrow ledge. She had her cell phone in her hand. He realized she was taking photos of the trail, the distance to the rocks and water below as well as the jagged rocky ledge's edge.

As she stepped closer to the edge, he heard a chunk of rock break off. It plummeted to the boulders below, and his heart fell with it. The rock shattered into pieces before dropping into the water pooling around the boulders, making ripples that lapped at the shore.

He felt his stomach roil. "Get down from there," he called up to her, his voice breaking. "Please." He couldn't watch. Sitting down again, he hung his head to keep from retching. It took a few minutes before his stomach settled and the need to vomit passed. When he looked up, Frankie was no longer balanced on the ledge.

His gaze shot to the rocks below, his pulse leaping with the horrible fear that filled him. There was no body on the rocks. No sign of Frankie. He put his head back down and took deep breaths. He didn't know how long he stayed like that before he heard the crunch of pine needles behind him.

"I'm sorry," Frankie said. "I should have known that would upset you."

He swore and started to get to his feet unsteadily. She held out a hand and he took it, letting her help him up. "I'm usually not like this."

She smiled. "You think I don't know that?"

"You should have told me you were going up there," he said.

"You would have tried to stop me," she said and pulled out her phone. "I needed to see it." She looked up from her screen. "Have you been up there?"

"Not since Naomi died, no."

She frowned, cocking her head. "You've jumped from there."

"When I was young and stupid."

Nodding, Frankie said, "You have to push off the cliff wall, throw your body out to miss

the rocks and to land in the pool. Daring thing
to do."

"Helps if you're young, stupid and with
other dumb kids who dare you," he said. "And
before you ask, yes, Naomi knew I'd jumped
off the ledge. She was terrified of heights. She
couldn't get three feet off the ground without having vertigo. It's why I know she didn't
climb up there on her own. Someone made
her."

"Sometimes people do things to try to overcome fears," Frankie said and shrugged.

"Naomi didn't. She was terrified of so
many things. Like horses. I tried to teach her
to ride." He shook his head. "I'm telling you,
she wouldn't have climbed up there unless
there was a gun to her head. Even if she'd
wanted to kill herself, she wouldn't have chosen that ledge as her swan song."

With that, he turned and started toward the
truck, wishing he'd never come back here.
He'd known it would be hard, but he hadn't
expected it to nearly incapacitate him. Had
he thought Naomi would be gone? Her soul
released? Not as long as her death was still a
mystery.

Frankie didn't speak again until they were
headed back toward Big Sky. "At some point

you're going to have to tell me why your father doesn't believe it was murder."

"I'll do one better. I'll get a copy of the case file. In the meantime, I'll show you Big Sky. I'm not ready for my parents to know the truth yet."

She nodded and leaned back as if to enjoy the trip. "I timed how long it took me to walk up the trail from the bridge to the ledge. Eleven minutes. How long do you think it would have taken Naomi?"

"Is this relevant?"

"It might be." She turned to look at him then. "You said the coroner established a time of death because of Naomi's broken wristwatch that was believed to have smashed on the rocks. We need to examine the time sequence. She left you at the ranch, right? The drive to the cliff took us ten minutes. She could have beat that because at that time of the evening in early fall and off season, there wouldn't have been as much traffic, right?"

He nodded.

"So if she left the ranch and went straight to the bridge—"

"She didn't. She met her killer at some point along the way. Maybe she stopped for gas or… I don't know. Picked up a hitchhiker."

Frankie shot him a surprised look. "From

what you've told me about Naomi, she wouldn't have stopped for a hitchhiker."

"It would have had to be someone she knew. Can we stop talking about this for just a little while?" He hated the pleading in his voice. "Let me show you around Big Sky, maybe drive up to Mountain Village."

She nodded and looked toward the town as he slowed for the turn. "So Big Sky was started by Montana native and NBC news co-anchorman Chet Huntley. I read it is the second-largest ski resort in the country by acreage." She gazed at Lone Mountain. "That peak alone stands at over eleven thousand feet."

He glanced over at her and chuckled. "You're like a walking encyclopedia. Do you always learn all these facts when you're… working?"

"Sure," she said, smiling. "I find it interesting. Like this canyon. There is so much history here. I've been trying to imagine this road when it was dirt and Yellowstone Park only accessible from here by horses and wagons or stagecoaches."

"I never took you for a history buff," he said.

She shrugged. "There's a lot you don't know about me."

He didn't doubt that, he thought as he studied her out of the corner of his eye. She continued to surprise him. She was so fearless. So different from Naomi. Just the thought of her up on that ledge— He shoved that thought away as he drove into the lower part of Big Sky known as Meadow Village. His mother was right. Big Sky had changed so much he hardly recognized the small resort town with all its restaurants and fancy shops along with miles of condos. He turned up the road to Mountain Village, where the ski resort was located, enjoying showing Frankie around. It kept his mind off Naomi.

"So you met the woman Hank brought home?"

Dana looked up at her sister, Stacy. They were in the ranch house kitchen, where Dana was taking cookies out of the oven. "I thought you might have run into them this morning before they took off for some sightseeing."

Her sister shook her head. Older than Dana, Stacy had been the wild one, putting several marriages under her belt at a young age. But she'd settled down after she'd had her daughter, Ella, and had moved back to the ranch to live in one of the new cabins up on the mountainside.

"I stopped over at their cabin this morning

to see if they needed anything," Stacy said now, avoiding her gaze.

Dana put her hands on her hips. She knew her sister so well. *"What?"*

Stacy looked up in surprise. "Nothing to get in a tizzy over, just something strange."

"Such as?"

"I don't want to be talking out of turn, but I noticed that they slept in separate bedrooms last night." Her sister snapped her lips shut as if the words had just sneaked out.

Dana frowned as she put another pan of cookie dough into the oven and, closing the door, set the timer. Hadn't she felt something between Hank and Frankie? Something not quite right? "They must have had a disagreement. I'm sure it is difficult for both of them being here after what happened with Naomi. That's bound to cause some tension between them."

"Probably. So, you like her?"

"I do. She's nothing like Naomi."

"What does that mean?" Stacy asked.

"There's nothing timid about her. She's more self-assured, seems more…independent. I was only around her for a little while. It's just an impression I got. You remember how Naomi was."

Her sister's right brow shot up. "You mean scared of everything?"

Dana had been so surprised the first time Hank had brought Naomi home and the young woman had no interest in learning to ride a horse.

I would be terrified to get on one, she'd said.

Naomi isn't...outdoorsy, was the way Hank had described her. That had been putting it mildly. Dana couldn't imagine the woman living here. As it turned out, living at Cardwell Ranch was the last thing Naomi had in mind.

"Frankie looks as if she can handle herself. I saw Hank gazing at her during dinner. He seems intrigued by her."

"I can't wait to meet her," Stacy said now.

"Why don't you come to dinner? Mary's going to be here, and Chase. Jordan and Liza are coming as well. I thought that was enough for one night." Her daughter and fiancé would keep things light. Her brother and his wife would be a good start as far as introducing Frankie to the family.

"Great. I'll come down early and help with the preparations," her sister said. "I'm sorry I mentioned anything about their sleeping arrangements. I'm sure it's nothing."

FRANKIE LOOKED OUT at the mountain ranges as she finished the lunch Hank had bought them up at the mountain resort. This was more like a vacation, something she hadn't had in years. She would have felt guilty except for the fact that technically she *was* working. She looked at the cowboy across the table from her, remembering the day he'd walked into her office in Lost Creek outside of Moscow, Idaho.

"Why now?" Frankie had asked him after he'd wanted to hire her to find out what had really happened to his girlfriend. "It's been three years, right? That makes it a cold case. I can't imagine there is anything to find." She'd seen that her words had upset him and had quickly lifted both hands in surrender. "I'm not saying it's impossible to solve a case that old…" She tried not to say the words *next to impossible*.

She'd talked him into sitting down, calming down and telling her about the crime. Turned out that the marshal—Hank's father—had sided with the coroner that the woman's death had been a suicide. She'd doubted this could get worse because it was clear to her that Hank Savage had been madly in love with the victim. Talk about wearing blinders. Of course he didn't want to believe the woman he loved had taken a nosedive off a cliff.

"I thought I could accept it, get over it," Hank had said. "I can't. I won't. I have to know the truth. I know this is going to sound crazy, but I can feel Naomi pleading with me to find her murderer."

It didn't sound crazy as much as it sounded like wishful thinking. If this woman had killed herself, then he blamed himself.

Her phone had rung. She'd checked to see who was calling and declined the call. But Hank could tell that the call had upset her.

"Look, if you need to take that…" he'd said.

"No." The last thing she wanted to do was take the call. What had her upset was that if she didn't answer one of the calls from the man soon, he would be breaking down her door. "So, what is it you want me to do?"

Hank had spelled it out for her.

She'd stared at him in disbelief. "You want me to go to Big Sky with you."

"I know it's a lot to ask and this might not be a good time for you."

He had no idea how good a time it was for her to leave town. "I can tell this is important for you. I can't make you any promises, but I'll come out and look into the incident." She'd pulled out her standard contract and slid it across the table with a pen.

Hank hadn't even bothered to read it. He'd

withdrawn his wallet. "Here's five hundred dollars. I'll pay all your expenses and a five-thousand-dollar bonus if you solve this case—along with your regular fee," he'd said, pushing the signed contract back across the table to her. As the same caller had rung her again, Hank had asked, "When can you leave?"

"Now's good," she'd said.

Chapter Five

Frankie had tried to relax during dinner later that night at the main ranch house, but it was difficult. She now understood at least the problem between Hank and his father. From what she could gather, the marshal was also angry with his son. Hank had refused to accept his father's conclusion about Naomi's death. The same conclusion the coroner had come up with as well.

Hank thought his father had taken the easy way out. But Frankie had been around Hud Savage only a matter of hours and she knew at gut level that he wasn't a man who took the easy way out. He believed clear to his soul that Naomi Hill had killed herself.

During dinner, Hank had said little. Dana's sister, Stacy, had joined them, along with Dana's daughter, Mary, and her fiancé, Chase, and Dana's brother, Jordan, and wife, Liza. Hank had been polite enough to his family, but she could tell he was struggling after going to the spot where Naomi had died.

She'd put a hand on his thigh to try to get him to relax and he'd flinched. The reaction hadn't gone unnoticed by his mother and aunt Stacy. Frankie had smiled and snuggled against him. If he hoped to keep their secret longer, he needed to be more attentive. After all, it was his idea that they pretend to be involved in a relationship. That way Frankie could look into Naomi's death without Hank going head-to-head with his father.

When she'd snuggled against him, he'd felt the nudge and responded, putting an arm around her and pulling her close. She'd whispered in his ear, "Easy, sweetie."

Nodding, he'd laughed, and she'd leaned toward him to kiss him on the lips. It had been a quick kiss meant to alleviate any doubt as to what was going on. The kiss had taken him by surprise. He'd stared into her eyes for a long moment, then smiled.

When Frankie had looked up, she'd seen there was relief on his mother's face. His mother had bought it. The aunt, not so much. But that was all right. The longer they could keep their ruse going, the better. Otherwise it would be war between father and son. They both wanted to avoid that since it hadn't done any good three years ago. Frankie doubted it would now.

"Cake?" Dana asked now, getting to her feet.

"I would love a piece," Frankie said. "Let me help you." She picked up her plate and Hank's to take them into the kitchen against his mother's protests. "You outdid yourself with dinner," she said as she put the dishes where the woman suggested.

Taking advantage of the two of them being alone with the door closed, Dana turned to her—just as Frankie had known she would. "I'm not being nosy, honestly. Is everything all right between you and Hank?"

She smiled as she leaned into the kitchen counter. She loved this kitchen with the warm yellow color, the photographs of family on the walls, the clichéd saying carved in the wood plaque hanging over the door. There was a feeling of permanency in this kitchen, in this house, this ranch. As if no matter what happened beyond that door, this place would weather the storm because it had survived other storms.

"It's hard on him being back here because of Naomi," Frankie said.

"Of course it is," Dana said on a relieved breath. "But he has you to help him through it."

She smiled and nodded. "I'm here for him and he knows it. Though it has put him on edge. But not to worry. I'll stand by him."

Tears filled the older woman's eyes as she quickly stepped to Frankie and threw her arms around her. "I can't tell you how happy I am that Hank has you."

She hadn't thought her generic words would cause such a response but she hugged Dana back, enjoying for a moment the warm hug from this genuine, open woman.

Dana stepped back, wiping her tears as Stacy and Jordan's wife, Liza, came in with the rest of the dirty dishes and leftover food. "We best get that cake out there or we'll have a riot on our hands," Dana said. "If you take the cake, I'll take the forks and dessert plates."

"I'M SORRY," HANK SAID when they reached their cabin and were finally alone again. Dinner had been unbearable, but he knew he should have played along better than he had. "You were great."

"Thanks. Your mother was worried we were having trouble. I assured her that coming back here is hard on you because of Naomi. Your family is nice," she said. "They obviously love you."

He groaned. He hated lying to his mother

most of all. "That's what makes this so hard. I wanted to burst out with the truth at dinner tonight." He could feel her gaze on him.

"Why didn't you?"

Hank shook his head. He thought about Frankie's kiss, her nuzzling against him. He'd known it would be necessary if they hoped to pass themselves off as a couple, but he hadn't been ready for it. The kiss had taken him by surprise. And an even bigger surprise had been his body's reaction to it, to her.

He turned away, glad it was late so they could go to bed soon. "I think I'm going to take a walk. Will you be all right here by yourself?"

She laughed. "I should think so since I'm trained in self-defense and I have a license to carry a firearm. You've never asked, but I'm an excellent shot."

"You have a gun?" He knew he shouldn't have been surprised and yet he was. She seemed too much like the girl next door to do the job she did. Slim, athletic, obviously in great shape, she just kept surprising him as to how good she was at this.

If anyone could find out the truth about Naomi, he thought it might be her.

AFTER HANK LEFT, Frankie pulled out her phone and looked again at the photographs she'd taken earlier from the ledge along the cliff. Standing up there being buffeted by the wind, her feet on the rocky ledge, she'd tried to imagine what Naomi had been thinking. If she'd had time to think.

Hank was so sure that she'd been murdered. It was such a strange way to murder someone. Also, she suspected there were other reasons his father believed it was suicide. The killer would have had to drag her up that trail from the bridge and then force her across the ledge. Dangerous, since if the woman was that terrified of heights, she would have grabbed on to her killer for dear life.

How had the killer kept her from pulling him down with her? It had been a male killer, hadn't it? That was what Frankie had imagined. Unless the couple hadn't gone up to the ledge with murder in mind.

Frankie rubbed her temples. People often did the thing you least expected them to do. Which brought her back to suicide. What if Hank was wrong? What if suicide was the only conclusion to be reached after this charade with his family? Would he finally be able to accept it?

The door opened and he came in on a warm summer night gust of mountain air. For a moment he was silhouetted, his broad shoulders filling the doorway. Then he stepped into the light, his handsome face twisted in grief. Her heart ached for him. She couldn't imagine the kind of undying love he'd felt for Naomi. Even after three years, he was still grieving. She wondered at the size of Hank's heart.

"I'd like to talk to Naomi's mother in the morning," she said, turning away from such raw pain. "Lillian Brandt, right?"

"Right." His voice sounded hoarse.

"It would help if you told me about the things that were going on with Naomi before her death, the things that made the coroner and your father believe it was a suicide." When he didn't answer, she turned. He was still standing just inside the door, his Stetson in the fingers of his left hand, his head down. She was startled for a moment and almost stepped to him to put her arms around him.

"There's something I haven't told you." He cleared his throat and looked up at her. "Naomi and I had a fight that night before she left the ranch." He swallowed.

She could see that this was going to take a while and motioned to the chairs as she turned and went into the small kitchen. Opening the refrigerator, she called over her shoulder, "Beer?" She pulled out two bottles even though she hadn't heard his answer and returned to the small living area.

He'd taken a seat, balancing on the edge, nervously turning the brim of his hat in his fingers. When she held out a beer, he took it and tossed his hat aside. Twisting off the cap, Frankie sat in the chair opposite him. She took a sip of the beer. It was icy cold and tasted wonderful. It seemed to soothe her and chase away her earlier thoughts when she'd seen Hank standing in the doorway.

She put her feet up on the well-used wooden coffee table, knowing her boots wouldn't be the first ones that had rested there. She wanted to provide an air of companionship to make it easier for him to tell her the truth. She'd learned this from her former cop uncle who'd been her mentor when she'd first started out.

"What did you fight about?" she asked as Hank picked at the label on his beer bottle with his thumb without taking a drink.

"It was stupid." He let out a bitter laugh as he lifted his head to meet her gaze. "I wasn't ready to get married and Naomi was." His voice broke again as he said, "She told me I was killing her."

Frankie took a drink of her beer before asking, "How long had you been going out?" It gave Hank a moment to collect himself.

He took a sip of his beer. "Since after college. We met on a blind date. She'd been working as an elementary school teacher, but said she'd rather be a mother and homemaker." He looked away. "I think that's what she wanted more than anything. Even more than me."

She heard something in his voice, in his words. "You didn't question that she loved you, did you?"

"No." He said it too quickly and then shook his head. "I did that night. I questioned a lot of things. She seemed so…so wrong for me. I mean, there was nothing about the ranch that she liked. Not the horses, the dust, the work. I'd majored in ranch management. I'd planned to come home after college and help my folks with the place."

"And that's what you were doing."

He nodded. "But Naomi didn't want to stay here. She didn't like the canyon or living on my folks' place. She wanted a home in a subdivision down in Bozeman. In what she called 'civilization with sidewalks.'" He shook his head. "I had no idea sidewalks meant that much to her before that night. She wanted everything I didn't."

"What did she expect you to do for a living in Bozeman?"

"Her stepfather had offered me a job. He

was a Realtor and he said he'd teach me the business." Hank took a long pull on his beer. "But I was a rancher. This is where I'd grown up. This is what I knew how to do and what I..."

"What you loved."

His blue eyes shone as they locked with hers. She saw that his pain was much deeper than even she'd thought. If Naomi had committed suicide, then he blamed himself because of the fight. He'd denied her what she wanted most, a different version of him.

"So she left hurt and angry," Frankie said. "Did she indicate where she was going? I'm assuming the two of you were living together here at the ranch."

"She said she was going to spend the night at her best friend Carrie White's apartment in Meadow Village here at Big Sky and that she needed time to think about all of this." He swallowed again. "I let her go without trying to fix it."

"It sounds like it wasn't an easy fix," Frankie commented and finished her beer. Getting up, she tilted the bottle in offer. Hank seemed to realize he still had a half-full bottle and quickly downed the rest. She took both empties to the kitchen and came back with two more.

Handing him one, she asked, "You tried to call her that night or the next morning?" As she asked the question, she knew where his parents would have stood on the marriage and Naomi issue. They wouldn't want to tarnish their son's relationship because of their opinions about his choice for a partner, but they also wouldn't want him marrying a woman who was clearly not a good match for him. One who took him off the ranch and the things he loved.

"That night, I was in no mood to discuss it further, so I waited and called her the next morning." He opened his beer and took a long pull. "Maybe if I'd called not long after she left—"

"What had you planned to say?" she asked, simply curious. It was a moot point now. Nor had his plans had anything to do with what happened to Naomi. By then, she was dead.

"I was going to tell her that I'd do whatever she wanted." He let out a long sigh and tipped the beer bottle to his lips. "But when she didn't answer, I changed my mind. I realized it wasn't going to work." His voice broke again. "I loved her, but she wanted to make me over, and I couldn't be the man she wanted me to be." His eyes narrowed. "You can dress me up, but underneath I'm still just a cowboy."

"Did you leave her a message on her phone?"

He nodded and looked away, his blue eyes glittering with tears. "I told her goodbye, but by then it would have been too late." His handsome face twisted in pain.

Frankie sat for a moment, considering everything he'd told her. "Was her cell phone found on her body or in her car?"

He shook his head. "Who knows what she did with it. The phone could have gone into the river. My father had his deputies search for it, but it was never found." His voice broke. "Maybe I did drive her to suicide," he said and took a drink as if to steady himself.

"I'm going to give you my professional opinion, for what it's worth," she said, knowing he wasn't going to like it. "I don't believe she killed herself. She knew that you loved her. She was just blowing off some steam when she headed for her friend's house. Did her friend see her at all?"

He shook his head.

"So she didn't go there. That would explain the discrepancy in the time she left you and when her watch was broken. Is there somewhere else she might have gone? Another friend's place? A male friend's?"

His eyes widened in surprise. "A male friend's? Why would you even ask about—"

"Because I know people. She was counting on you to change and do what she wanted, but after four years? She would have realized it was a losing battle and had someone else waiting in the wings."

He slammed down his beer bottle and shoved to his feet. "You make her sound like she was—"

"A woman determined to get married, have kids, stay home and raise them while her husband had a good job that allowed all her dreams to come true?"

"She wasn't—she—" He seemed at a loss for words.

"Hey, Hank. Naomi was a beautiful woman who had her own dreams." He had showed her a photograph of Naomi. Blonde, green-eyed, a natural beauty.

Ignoring a strange feeling of jealousy, Frankie got to her feet and finished her beer before she spoke. She realized that she'd probably been too honest with him. But someone needed to be, she told herself. It wasn't just the beer talking. Or that sudden stab of jealousy when she'd thought of Naomi.

In truth, she was annoyed at him because she knew that if he'd reached Naomi on the phone that night, he would have buckled under. He would have done whatever she wanted, including marrying her. On some level, he would have been miserable and resented her the rest of his life, but being the man he was, he would have made the best of it. Naomi dying had saved him and he didn't even realize it.

"We need to find the other man," Frankie said as she took her bottle to the recycling bin before turning toward the bedroom.

Hank let out a curse. "You're wrong. You're dead wrong. I don't know why I—"

She cut off the rest of his words as she closed the bedroom door. She knew he was angry and probably ready to fire her. All she could hope was that he would cool down by the morning and would trust that she knew what she was talking about. Oh, she'd known women like Naomi all her life—including her very own mother, who chewed up men and spit them out one after another as they disappointed her. That was the problem with trying to make over a man.

HANK COULDN'T SLEEP. He lay in the second bedroom, staring up at the ceiling, cursing the fact that he'd brought Frankie here. What had he been thinking? This had to be the stupidest idea he'd ever come up with. Clearly, she didn't get it. She hadn't known Naomi.

Another man?

He thought about storming into her bedroom, telling her to pack her stuff and taking her back to Idaho tonight. Instead, he tossed and turned, getting more angry by the hour. He would fire her. First thing in the morning, he'd do just that.

Who did she think she was, judging Naomi like that? Naomi was sweet, gentle, maybe a little too timid… He rolled over and glared at the bedroom door. Another man in the wings! The thought made him so angry he could snap off nails with his teeth.

As his blood pressure finally began to drop somewhere around midnight, he found himself wondering if Naomi's friend Carrie knew more than she'd originally told him. If there had been another man—

He gave that thought a hard shove away. Naomi had loved him. Only him. She'd wanted the best for him. He rolled over again. She thought she knew what was best for him. He kicked at the blanket tangled around his legs. Maybe if she had lived she would have realized that what was best for him, for them, was staying on the ranch, letting him do what he knew and loved. Sidewalks were overrated.

Staring up at the ceiling, he felt the weight of her death press against his chest so hard that for a moment he couldn't breathe.

You don't want to let yourself believe that she committed suicide because you feel guilty about the argument you had with her before she left the ranch, his father had said. *Son, believe me, it took more than some silly argument for her to do what she did. We often don't know those closest to us or what drives them to do what they do. This wasn't your fault.*

Hank groaned, remembering his father's words three years ago. Could he be wrong about a lot of things? He heard the bedroom door open. He could see Frankie silhouetted in the doorway.

"If there is another man, then it would prove that she didn't commit suicide," the PI said. The bedroom door closed.

He glared at it for a long moment. Even if Frankie had gone back to her bedroom and locked the door, he knew he could kick it down if he wanted to. But as Frankie's words registered, he pulled the blanket up over him and closed his eyes, exhausted from all of this.

If there had been another man, then he would be right about her being murdered.

Was that supposed to give him comfort?

Chapter Six

"I told my mother that we were having breakfast in town," Hank said when Frankie came out of the bedroom fully dressed and showered the next morning. He had his jacket on and smelled of the outdoors, which she figured meant he'd walked down to the main house to talk to his mother.

"I'm going to take a shower," he said now. "If you want to talk to Naomi's mother, we need to catch her before she goes to work." With that, he turned and went back into his bedroom.

Frankie smiled after him. He was still angry but he hadn't fired her. Yet.

She went into the kitchen and made herself toast. Hank didn't take long in the shower. He appeared minutes later, dressed in jeans and a Western shirt, his dark, unruly hair still damp at his collar as he stuffed on his Stetson and headed for the door. She followed, smiling

to herself. It could be a long day, but she was
glad she was still employed for numerous reasons, number one among them, she wanted to
know now more than ever what had happened
to Naomi Hill.

Lillian Brandt lived in a large condo complex set back against a mountainside overlooking Meadow Village. She'd married a
real-estate agent after being a single mother
for years, from what Hank had told her. Big
Sky was booming and had been for years, so
Lillian had apparently risen in economic stat-
ure after her marriage compared to the way
she'd lived before Naomi died.

From her research, Frankie knew that Big
Sky, Montana, once a ranching area, had been
nothing more than a sagebrush-filled meadow
below Lone Mountain. Then Chet Huntley
and some developers had started the resort.
Since then, the sagebrush had been plowed up
to make a town as the ski resort on the mountain had grown.

But every resort needed workers, and while
million-dollar houses had been built, there
were few places for moderate-income workers to live that they could afford. The major-
ity commuted from Gallatin Gateway, Four
Corners, Belgrade and Bozeman—all towns
forty miles or more to the north.

Lillian was younger than Frankie had expected. Naomi had been four years younger than Hank. Frankie estimated that Lillian must have had her daughter while in her late teens.

"Hank?" The woman's pale green eyes widened in surprise. "Are you back?"

"For a while," he said and introduced Frankie. "Do you have a minute? We won't take much of your time."

Lillian looked from him to Frankie and back before she stepped aside to let them enter the condo. It was bright and spacious with no clutter. It could have been one of the models that real-estate agents showed prospective clients. "I was just about to leave to go to the office." She worked for her husband as a secretary.

"I just need to ask you a few questions," he said as she motioned for them to take a seat.

"Questions?" she asked as she moved some of the pillows on the couch to make room for them.

"About Naomi's death."

The woman stopped what she was doing to stare at him. "Hank, it's been three years. Why would you dig all of it back up again?"

"Because he doesn't believe she killed herself," Frankie said and supplied her business card. "I didn't know your daughter, but I've heard a lot about her. I'm sorry for your loss, ma'am." Then she asked if it would be okay if Mrs. Brandt would answer a few questions about her daughter. "She was twenty-six, right? Hank said she was ready to get married."

Lillian slumped into one of the chairs that she'd freed of designer pillows and motioned them onto the couch. "It's all she wanted. Marriage, a family."

"Where was she working at the time of her death?" Frankie asked.

"At the grocery store, but I can't see what that—"

She could feel Hank's gaze on her. "Is that where she met her friend Carrie?"

Lillian nodded. Her gaze went to Hank. "Why are you—"

"I'm curious," Frankie said, drawing the woman's attention back again. "Was there anyone else in her life?"

"You mean friends?"

"Yes, possibly a male friend," Frankie said.

The woman blinked before shooting a look at Hank. "She was in love with Hank."

"But she had to have other friends."

Lillian fiddled with the piping along the

edge of the chair arm. "Of course she had other friends. She made friends easily."

"I'm sure she did. She was so beautiful," Frankie said.

The woman nodded, her eyes shiny. "She got asked out a lot all through school."

"Do you remember their names?"

Lillian looked at Hank. "She was faithful to you. If that's what this is about—"

"It's not," Hank assured her.

"We just thought they might be able to fill in some of the blanks so Hank can better understand what happened to Naomi. He's having a very hard time moving on," Frankie said.

The woman looked at Hank, sympathy in her gaze. "Of course. I just remember her mentioning one in particular. His name was—" she seemed to think for a moment "— River." She waved her hand wistfully. "Blame it on Montana, these odd names."

"You probably don't remember River's last name," Frankie said.

"No, but Carrie might. She knew him too." Lillian looked at her watch. "I really have to go. I'm sorry."

"No," Frankie said, getting to her feet. "You've been a great help."

"Yes," Hank agreed with much less enthusiasm. "Thank you for taking the time."

"It's good to see you," the woman said to him and patted his cheek. "I hope you can find some peace."

"Me too," he said as he shared a last hug with Mrs. Brandt before leaving.

HANK CLIMBED BEHIND the wheel, his heart hammering in his chest. "You aren't going to give up on your other man theory, are you?"

"No, and you shouldn't either," Frankie said from the passenger seat.

He finally turned his head to look at her. Gritting his teeth, he said, "You think she was cheating on me? Wouldn't that give me a motive for murder?"

"I don't think she was cheating. I said she had someone waiting in the wings. Big Sky is a small town. I suspect that if she'd been cheating on you, you would have heard."

"Thanks. You just keep making me feel better all the time."

"I didn't realize that my job was to make you feel better. I thought it was to find a killer."

He let out a bark of a laugh. "You are something, you know that?"

"It's been mentioned to me. I'm hungry. Are you going to feed me before or after we visit Naomi's best friend, Carrie?"

"I'm not sure I can do this on an empty stomach, so I guess it's going to be before," he said as he started the pickup's engine.

"Over breakfast, you can tell me about Carrie," she said as she buckled up.

"I don't know what you want me to tell you about her," he grumbled, wishing he'd gone with his instincts last night and stormed into her bedroom and fired her. Even if he'd had to kick down the door.

"Start by telling me why you didn't like her."

He shot her a look as he pulled away from the condo complex. "What makes you think…?" He swore under his breath. "Don't you want to meet her and decide on your own?"

"Oh, I will. But I'm curious about your relationship with her."

Hank let out a curse as he drove toward a local café off the beaten path. The place served Mexican breakfasts, and he had a feeling Frankie liked things hot. She certainly got him hot under his collar.

It wasn't until they were seated and had ordered—he'd been right about her liking spicy food—that he sat back and studied the woman sitting across from him.

"What?" she asked, seeming to squirm a little under his intent gaze.

"Just that you know everything about me—"

"Not everything."

"—and I know nothing about you," he finished.

"That's because this isn't about me," she said and straightened her silverware. He'd never seen her nervous before. But then again, he'd never asked her anything personal about herself.

"You jumped at this case rather fast," he said, still studying her. She wasn't the only one who noticed things about people. "I suspect it was to avoid whoever that was who kept calling you." He saw that he'd hit a nerve. "Angry client? Old boyfriend?" He grinned. "Old boyfriend."

"You're barking up the wrong tree."

"Am I? I don't think so." He took her measure for the first time since he'd hired her. She was a very attractive woman. Right now her long, dark hair was pulled back into a low ponytail. Sans makeup, she'd also played down the violet eyes. And yet there was something sexy and, yes, even sultry about her. Naomi wouldn't leave the house without her makeup on.

That thought reminded him of all the times

he'd stood around waiting for her to get ready to go out.

This morning Frankie was more serious, more professional, more hands-off. Definitely low-maintenance in a simple T-shirt and jeans. Nothing too tight. Nothing too revealing.

And yet last night at dinner when she'd snuggled against him, he'd felt her full curves. Nothing could hide her long legs. Right now, he could imagine her contours given that she was slim and her T-shirt did little to hide the curve of her backside.

"Why isn't a woman who looks like you married?" he asked, truly surprised.

"Who says I'm not?"

He glanced at her left hand. "No ring."

She smiled and looked away for a moment. "Isn't it possible I'm just not wearing mine right now?"

Hank considered that as the waitress brought their breakfasts. "*Are* you married?" he asked as the waitress left again.

"No. Now, are you going to tell me why you didn't like Naomi's best friend or are you going to keep stalling?"

Chapter Seven

Johnny Joe "J.J." Whitaker tried the number again. Frankie hadn't been picking up, but now all his calls were going to voice mail. Did she really think he would quit calling? The woman didn't know him very well if she did. That was what made him so angry. She *should* know him by now. He wasn't giving up.

He left another threatening message. "Frankie, you call me or you're going to be sorry. You know I make good on my threats, sweetheart. Call me or you'll wish you had."

He hung up and paced the floor until he couldn't take it anymore. She had to have gotten his messages. She had to know what would happen if she ignored him.

He slammed his fist down on the table, and the empty beer bottles from last night rattled. One toppled over, rolled across the table and would have fallen to the floor if he hadn't caught it.

"Frankie, you bitch!" he screamed, grabbing the neck of the bottle. He brought the bottle down on the edge of the table.

The bottom end of the bottle broke off, leaving a lethal jagged edge below the neck in his hand. He held it up in the light and imagined what the sharp glass could do to a person's flesh. Frankie thought he was dangerous?

He laughed. Maybe it was time to show her just how dangerous he could be.

CARRIE WHITE HAD gotten married not long after Naomi died, Hank told her on the way over to the woman's house. She had been about Naomi's age, and they'd met at the grocery store where Naomi had worked. Carrie had worked at one of the art shops in town. They became friends.

"Was she a bad influence?" Frankie asked.

Hank shrugged. "I don't know."

"How was Carrie with men?"

"She always had one or two she was stringing along, hoping one of them would pop the question."

Frankie laughed. "Is this why you didn't like her?"

"I never said I didn't like her. I just didn't think she was good for Naomi. You have to understand. Naomi was raised by her mother.

Her father left when she was six. It devastated her. Lillian had to go to work and raise her alone without any more education than a high school diploma."

"So they didn't have much money?"

"Or anything else. Naomi wanted more and I don't blame her for that."

"Also Naomi didn't want to end up like her," Frankie supposed.

"She wanted a husband, a family, some stability. When her mother started dating the real-estate agent, she wanted that for us."

"Seems pretty stable at the ranch," Frankie said.

"I would have been working for my parents. Naomi couldn't see how I would ever get ahead since even if they left me the ranch, I still have a sister, Mary, and two younger brothers, Brick and Angus. I could see her point. She wanted her own place, her own life, that wasn't tied up with my family's."

Frankie held her tongue. The more she found out about Naomi, the more she could see how she would not have been in the right place emotionally to be involved in a serious relationship. But she was having these thoughts because the more she learned about Hank, the more she liked him.

"So Carrie encouraged her how?"

Hank seemed to give that some thought as he pulled up in front of a small house in a subdivision in Meadow Village. "Carrie encouraged her to dump me and find someone else, someone more...acceptable. Carrie married a local insurance salesman who wears a three-piece suit most days unless he's selling to out-of-staters, and then he busts out his Stetson and boots."

Frankie got the picture. She opened her door, anxious to meet Carrie White and see what she thought of her for herself. She heard Hank get out but could tell that he wasn't looking forward to this.

At the front door, Frankie rang the bell. She could hear the sound of small running feet, then a shriek of laughter followed by someone young bursting into tears.

"Knock it off!" yelled an adult female voice.

She could hear someone coming to the door. It sounded as if the person was dragging one of the crying children because now there appeared to be at least two in tears just on the other side of the door.

"Naomi's dream life?" she said under her breath to Hank.

The woman who opened the door with a toddler on one arm and another hanging off her pants leg looked harried and near tears herself. Carrie was short, dark-haired and still carrying some of her baby weight. She frowned at them and said, "Whatever you're offering, I'm not inter—" Her voice suddenly broke off at the sight of Hank. Her jaw literally dropped.

"Fortunately, we aren't selling anything," Frankie said.

"We'd just like a minute of your time," Hank said as the din died down. The squalling child hanging off Carrie's leg was now staring at them, just like the toddler on her hip. "Mind if we come in?"

The woman shot a look at Frankie, then shrugged and shoved open the screen door. "Let me just put them down for their morning naps. Have a seat," she said over her shoulder as she disappeared down a hallway.

The living room looked like a toy manufacturing company had exploded and most of the toys had landed here in pieces. Against one wall by the door was a row of hooks. Frankie noticed there were a half-dozen sizes of coats hanging there.

They waded through the toys, cleaning off a space on the couch to sit down. In the other room they could hear cajoling and more crying, but pretty soon, Carrie returned.

Frankie could see that she'd brushed her

hair and put on a little makeup in a rush and changed her sweatshirt for one that didn't have spit-up on it. The woman was making an effort to look as if everything was fine. Clearly the attempt was for Hank's benefit.

"It's so good to see you," Carrie said to him, still looking surprised that he'd somehow ended up on her couch.

Frankie guessed that things had not been good between Carrie and Hank after Naomi's death. It seemed Carrie regretted that.

"How have you been?" she asked as she cleared toys off a chair and sat down. She looked exhausted and the day was early.

"All right," he said. "We need to ask you some questions."

The woman stiffened a little. She must have thought this was a social call. "Questions about what?"

"I understand you didn't see or hear from Naomi the night she died," Frankie said. Carrie looked at her and then at Hank.

He said, "This is Frankie, a private investigator. She's helping me find out what happened that night."

The woman turned again to her, curiosity in her gaze, but she didn't ask about their relationship. "I've told you everything I know," she said to Hank before turning back to Frankie. "I didn't hear from her or see her. I told the marshal the same thing."

"Were you planning to?"

The question seemed to take Carrie off guard. "I can't…" She frowned.

"Hadn't your best friend told you that she was going to push marriage that night and if Hank didn't come around…"

The woman's eyes widened. "I wouldn't say she was pushing marriage exactly. It had been four years! How long does it take for a man to make up his mind?" She slid a look at Hank and flushed a little with embarrassment.

"How long did it take your husband?"

Carrie ran a hand through her short hair. "Six months."

Frankie eyed her, remembering the coats hanging on the hooks by the door. "Were you pregnant?"

The woman shot to her feet, her gaze ricocheting back to Hank. "I don't know what this is about, but—"

"She was your best friend. You knew her better than anyone," Frankie said, also getting to her feet. "She would have told you if there was someone else she was interested in. I'm guessing she planned to come back to your place that night if things didn't go well. Unless you weren't such good friends."

Carrie crossed her arms. "She was my *best* friend."

"Then she would have told you about River."

That caught the woman flat-footed. She blinked, looked at Hank again and back to Frankie. "It was Hank's own fault. He kept dragging his feet."

She nodded. "So Naomi must have called to tell you she was on her way."

Carrie shook her head. "I told you. I didn't see her. I didn't hear from her. When I didn't, I just assumed everything went well. Until I got the call the next morning from her mother."

Frankie thought the woman was telling the truth. But Naomi would have called someone she trusted. Someone she could pour her heart out to since she left the ranch upset. "Where can we find River?"

HANK SWORE AS he climbed into his pickup. "I don't want to go see River Dean," he said as Frankie slid into the passenger seat.

"After Naomi left you, she would have gone to one of two places. Carrie's to cry on her shoulder. Or someone else's shoulder. If the man waiting in the wings was River Dean, then that's where she probably went. Which means he might have been the last person to see her alive. If he turned her down as well, maybe she did lose all hope and make that fatal leap from the cliff. You ready to accept that and call it a day?"

Without looking at her, Hank jerked off his Stetson to rake a hand through his hair. "You scare me."

"She wanted to get married and have babies and a man who came home at five thirty every weekday night and took off his tie as she gave him a cocktail and a kiss and they laughed about the funny things the kids had done that day. It's a fantasy a lot of people have."

He stared at her. "But not you."

She shrugged.

"Because you know the fantasy doesn't exist," he said, wanting to reach over and brush back a lock of dark hair that had escaped from her ponytail and now curled across her cheek.

"I'm practical, but even I still believe in love and happy-ever-after."

Surprised, he did reach over and push back the lock of hair. His fingertips brushed her cheek. He felt a tingle run up his arm. Frankie caught his hand and held it for a moment before letting it go. He could see that he'd invaded her space and it had surprised her. It hadn't pleased her.

"You said you wanted the truth," she reminded him, as if his touching her had been an attempt to change the subject. "Have you changed your mind?"

RIVER DEAN OWNED a white-water rafting company that operated downriver closer to what was known as the Mad Mile and House Rock, an area known for thrills and spills.

Frankie could still feel where Hank's fingertips had brushed her cheek. She wanted to reach up and rub the spot. But she resisted just as she had the shudder she'd felt at his sudden touch.

Hank got out of the pickup and stopped in front of a makeshift-looking building with a sign that read WHITE-WATER RAFTING.

The door was open, and inside she could see racks of life jackets hanging from the wall. A motorcycle was parked to one side of the building. Someone was definitely here since there was also a huge stack of rafts in the pine trees, only some of them still chained to a tree. It was early in the day, so she figured business picked up later.

All she could think was that Naomi was foolish enough to trade ranch life for this? A seasonal business determined by the weather and tourists passing through? But maybe three years ago, River Dean had appeared to have better options. And if not, there was always Naomi's stepfather and the real-estate business.

Hank stood waiting for her, staring at the river through the pines. She felt the weight of her cell phone and her past. She'd turned off her phone earlier, but now she pulled it out and checked to see that she had a dozen calls from the same number. No big surprise. She didn't even consider checking voice mail since she knew what she'd find. He'd go by the office and her apartment—if he hadn't already. He would know that she'd left town. She told herself he wouldn't be able to find her even if he tried. Unfortunately, he would try, and if he got lucky somehow…

"You ready?" Hank said beside her.

She pocketed her phone. "Ready as *you* are."

He chuckled at that and started toward the open door of the white-water rafting business. She followed.

The moment she walked in she spotted River Dean. She'd known men like him in Idaho. Good-looking ski bums, mountain bikers, river rafters. Big Sky resembled any resort area with its young men who liked to play.

River Dean was tanned and athletically built with shaggy, sexy blond hair and a million-dollar smile. She saw quickly how a woman would have been attracted to him. It wasn't until she approached him that she could tell his age was closer to forty than thirty. There were lines around his eyes from hours on the water in sunshine.

Hank had stopped just inside the door and was staring at River as if he wanted to rip his throat out.

"You must be River," she said, stepping in front of Hank. River appeared to be alone. She got the feeling that he'd just sent some employees out with a couple of rafts full of adventure seekers.

"Wanting a trip down the river?" he asked, grinning at her and then Hank. His grin faded a little as if he recognized the cowboy rancher Naomi had been dating.

"More interested in your relationship with Naomi Hill," Frankie said.

"You a…cop?" he asked, eyeing her up and down.

"Something like that. Naomi came to see you that night, the night she died."

River shook his head. "I don't know who

you are, but I'm not answering any more of your questions."

"Would you prefer to talk to the sheriff?" Frankie snapped.

"No, but…"

"We're just trying to find out what happened to her. I know she came to see you. She was upset. She needed someone to talk to. Someone sympathetic to her problem."

River rubbed the back of his neck for a moment as he looked toward the open door and the highway outside. She could tell he was wishing a customer would stop by right now.

"We know you knew her," Hank said, taking a threatening step forward.

River was shaking his head. "It wasn't like that. I was way too old for her. We were just friends. And I swear I know nothing about what happened to her."

"But she did stop by that night," Frankie repeated.

The river guide groaned. "She stopped by, but I was busy."

"Busy?" Hank said.

"With another woman." Frankie nodded since she'd already guessed that was what must have happened. "Did you two argue?"

"No." He held up his hands. "I told her we

could talk the next day. She realized what was going on and left. That was it," River said.

Hank swore. "But you didn't go to the sheriff with that information even though you might have been the last person to see her alive."

"I wasn't why she jumped," River snapped. "If you're looking for someone to blame, look in the mirror, man. You're the one who was making her so unhappy."

Frankie could see that Hank wanted to reach across the counter and thump the man. She stepped between them again. "Tell me what was said that night."

River shook his head. "It was three years ago. I don't remember word for word. She surprised me. She'd never come by before without calling."

Behind her, Frankie heard Hank groan. River heard it too and looked worried. Both men were strong and in good shape, but Hank was a big cowboy. In a fight, she had no doubt that the cowboy would win.

"It's like I just told you. She was upset before she saw what was going on. I told her she had to leave and that we'd talk the next day. She was crying, but she seemed okay when she left."

"This was at your place? Where was that?"

"I was staying in those old cabins near Soldiers' Chapel. Most of them have been torn down since then."

"Did you see her leave?" Frankie asked. "Could she have left with anyone?"

River shook his head and looked sheepish. "Like I said. I thought she was all right. I figured she was looking for a shoulder to cry on over her boyfriend and that she'd just find someone else to talk to that night."

"Was there someone you thought she might go to?" she asked.

River hesitated only a moment before he said, "Her friend Carrie maybe? I don't know."

Chapter Eight

"You should have let me hit him," Hank said as he slipped behind the wheel and slammed the door harder than he'd meant to.

"Violence is never the answer."

He shot her a look. "You read that in a fortune cookie?" He couldn't help himself. He couldn't remember the last time he was this angry.

He saw Frankie's expression and swore under his breath. "Yes, I'd prefer to blame River Dean rather than the dead woman I was in love with. You have a problem with that?"

She said nothing, as if waiting for his anger to pass. His father had warned him that digging into Naomi's death would only make him feel worse. He really hated it when his father was right—and Hud didn't even know that was what he was doing.

He drove back to the ranch, his temper cooled as he turned into the place.

"I had no idea about what was going on with Naomi," he said, stating the obvious. "You must think me a fool."

Frankie graced him with a patient smile as he drove down the road to the ranch house. "She loved you, but you both wanted different things. Love doesn't always overcome everything."

"Don't be nice to me," he said gruffly, making her laugh. Her cell phone rang. She checked it as if surprised that she'd left it on and quickly turned it off again.

"You're going to have to talk to him sometime," Hank said, studying her.

"Is there anyone else you want to go see?"

He shook his head, aware that she'd circumvented his comment as he parked at the foot of the trail that led to their cabin on the mountainside. "I need to be alone for a while, Frankie. Is that all right?"

"Don't worry about me."

He smiled at her. "You can take care of yourself, right? Never need any help."

"I wouldn't say that." She opened her door and got out.

He swore and, after throwing the pickup into Park, got out and went after her. "Frankie, wait."

She stopped and turned back to him.

"I don't know what your story is, but I do know this," he said. "You have closed yourself off for some reason. I recognize the signs because I've done it for the past three years. In your case, I suspect some man's to blame, the one who keeps calling. One question. Is he dangerous?"

She started to step away, but he reached for her arm and pulled her back around to face him again. "I'm fine. There is nothing to worry about."

He shook his head but let go of her arm. "You are one stubborn woman." He couldn't help but smile because there was a strength and independence in her that he admired. He'd never known a woman quite like her. She couldn't have been more different from Naomi, who he'd always felt needed taking care of. Just the thought of Naomi and what he'd learned about her before she died was like a bucket of ice water poured over him. He took a step away, needing space right now, just like he'd told her.

"I'll see you later." With that, he turned to his pickup and drove off, looking back only once to see Frankie standing in the ranch yard, a worried expression on her face.

"Nothing to worry about, huh?" he said under his breath.

AS FRANKIE TURNED toward their cabin on the mountain, she saw movement in the main house and knew that their little scene had been witnessed. They didn't appear to be a loving couple. She didn't know how much longer they could continue this ruse before someone brought it up.

But this was the way Hank wanted it. At least for the time being. She felt guilty, especially about his mother. Dana wanted her son to move on from Naomi's death and find some happiness. Frankie wasn't sure that was ever going to happen.

She hated to admit it to herself, but the moment Hank had told her about the problems they'd been having, she'd nailed the kind of young woman Naomi had been.

The weight of her cell phone in her pocket seemed to mock her. She was good at figuring out *other* people, but not so good when it came to her own life.

"Frankie!" She turned at the sound of Dana's voice. The older woman was standing on the ranch house porch, waving at her. "Want a cup of coffee? I have cookies."

She couldn't help but laugh as she started for the main house. Dana wanted to talk and she was using cookies as a bribe. Frankie called her on it the moment she reached the porch.

"You've found me out," Dana said with a laugh. "I'll stoop to just about anything when it comes to my son."

"I understand completely," she said, climbing the steps to the porch. "Hank is a special young man."

"Yes, I think he is," the woman said as she shoved open the screen door. "I thought we could talk."

Frankie chuckled. "I had a feeling." She stepped inside, taking in again the Western-style living room with its stone fireplace, wood floors, and Native American rugs adjacent to the warm and cozy kitchen. She liked it here, actually felt at home, which was unusual for her. She often didn't feel at home at her own place.

"I never asked," Dana said as she filled two mugs with coffee, handed one to Frankie and put a plate of cookies on the table. "How did you two meet?" She motioned her into a chair.

Hank hired me to pretend to be his girlfriend. "At a bar." It was the simplest answer she could come up with. She wondered why she and Hank hadn't covered this part. They should have guessed at least his mother would ask.

"Really? That surprises me. I've never known Hank to be interested in the bar scene and he isn't much of a drinker, is he?" Dana let out an embarrassed laugh. "I have to keep reminding myself that he's been gone three years. Maybe I don't really know my son anymore."

Frankie chuckled and shook her head. "Hank only came into the bar to pick up some dinner. Apparently it had been a long day at work and he'd heard that we served the best burgers in Idaho. I just happened to be working that night, and since it was slow, we got to talking. A few days later, he tracked me down because I was only filling in at the bar. A friend of mine owns it. Anyway, Hank asked me out and the rest is history."

It was pure fiction, but it was what she saw Dana needed to hear. Hank was no bar hound. Still, she felt guilty even making up such a story. It would have been so much easier to tell the truth. But her client had been adamant about them keeping the secret as long as they could.

Dana took a sip of her coffee and then asked, "So when not helping a friend, what do you do?"

"I'm a glorified secretary for a boss who makes me work long hours." That at least felt like the truth a lot of days. "Seriously, I love my job and my boss is okay most of the time. But I spend a lot of time doing paperwork."

"Oh my, well, you must be good at it. I'm terrible at it. That's why it is such a blessing that our Mary stayed around and does all of the accounting for the ranch."

"These cookies are delicious," Frankie said, taking a bite of one. "I would love your recipe." The diversion worked as she'd hoped. Dana hopped up to get her recipe file and began to write down the ingredients and explain that the trick was not to overbake them.

"So you cook," Dana said, kicking the conversation off into their favorite recipes. Frankie had no trouble talking food since she did cook and she had wonderful recipes that her grandmother had left her.

FRUSTRATED AND ANGRY at himself and Naomi, Hank drove out of the ranch, not sure where he was going. All he knew was that he wanted to be alone for a while.

But as he turned onto the highway, he knew exactly where he was headed. Back to the river. Back to the cliff and the ledge where she'd jumped. Back to that deep, dark, cold pool and the rocks where her body had been found.

He knew there was nothing to find there

and yet he couldn't stay away. It was one of the reasons he'd left after Naomi died. That and his grief, his unhappiness, his anger at his father.

After pulling off the road, he wound back into the pines and parked. For a moment he sat behind the wheel, looking out at the cliff through the trees. What did he hope to find here? Shaking his head, he climbed out and walked through the pines to the rocky shore of the river. Afternoon sunlight poured down through the boughs, making the surface of the river shimmer.

A cool breeze ruffled his hair as he sat down on a large rock. Shadows played on the cliff across from him. When he looked up at the ledge, just for a moment he thought he saw Naomi in her favorite pale yellow dress, the fabric fluttering in the wind as she fell.

He blinked and felt his eyes burn with tears. Frankie was right. He and Naomi had wanted different things. They hadn't been right for each other, but realizing that didn't seem to help. He couldn't shake this feeling he'd had for three years. It was as if she was trying to reach him from the grave, pleading with him that he find her killer.

Hank pulled off his Stetson and raked a hand through his hair. Was it just guilt for not marrying her, not taking the job with her stepfather, not giving up the ranch for her? Or was it true? Had she been murdered?

He reminded himself that this was why he was back here. Why he'd gone to Frankie to begin with and talked her into this charade. He realized, as he put his hat back on to shade his eyes from the summer sun, he trusted Frankie to find out the truth. Look how much she'd discovered so far. He told himself it was a matter of time. If they could just keep their…relationship secret…

At the sound of a twig breaking behind him, Hank swung around, startled since he'd thought he was alone. Through the pines he saw a flash of color as someone took off at a run.

He jumped to his feet, but had to work his way back through the rocks, so he couldn't move as fast. By the time he reached the pines, whoever it had been was gone. He told himself it was probably just a kid who was as startled as he was to see that there was someone at this spot.

But as he stood, trying to catch his breath, he knew it hadn't been a kid. The person had been wearing a light color. The same pale yellow as Naomi's favorite dress or just his imagination? He'd almost convinced himself that he'd seen a ghost until, in the distance, he heard the sound of a vehicle engine rev and then die away.

Chapter Nine

After her visit with Dana, Frankie realized
that she and Hank had to move faster. His
mother was no fool. Frankie could tell that
she was worried.

"Is there a vehicle I could borrow?" Frankie
asked after their coffee and cookies chat.

"Of course." Dana had moved to some
hooks near the door and pulled down a set of
keys. "These are to that blue pickup out there.
You're welcome to use it anytime you like.
Hank should have thought of that. Where did
he go, anyway?"

"He had some errands to run and I didn't
want to go along. I told him I would be fine
exploring. I think I'll go into town and run a
few errands of my own." She gave the woman
what she hoped was a reassuring smile and
took the keys and the pickup to head into
town.

Frankie felt an urgency to finish this. It

wasn't just because their pretense was going to be found out sooner rather than later. Nor was it because she'd left a lot of things unfinished back in Idaho, though true. It was being here, pretending to be in love with Hank, pretending that there was a chance that she could be part of this amazing family at some time in the future.

That, she knew, was the real problem. Hank was the kind of man who grew on a woman. But with his family, she'd felt instant love and acceptance. She didn't want to hurt these people any longer. That meant solving this case and getting out of here.

At the local grocery store, she found the manager in the back. She'd assumed that after three years, the managers would have changed from when Naomi had worked here. She was wrong.

Roy Danbrook was a tall, skinny man of about fifty with dark hair and eyes. He rose from his chair, looked around his incredibly small office as if surprised how small it really was and then invited her in. She took the plastic chair he offered her, feeling as if being in the cramped place was a little too intimate. But this wouldn't take long.

"I'm inquiring about a former worker of

yours, Naomi Hill," she said, ready to lie about her credentials if necessary.

Roy frowned and she realized he probably didn't even remember Naomi after all this time. The turnover in resort towns had to be huge.

"Naomi," he said and nodded. "You mentioned something about an insurance claim?"

She nodded. She'd flashed him her PI credentials, but he'd barely looked at them. "I need to know what kind of employee she was."

He seemed to think for a moment. "Sweet, very polite with customers…" She felt a *but* coming. "But I had no choice but to let her go under the circumstances."

This came as a surprise. Did Hank know Naomi had been fired? "The circumstances?" That could cover a lot of things.

The manager looked away for a moment, clearly uncomfortable with speaking of past employees, or of the dead? "The stealing." He shook his head.

"The stealing?" All she could think of was groceries.

"Unfortunately, she couldn't keep her hand out of the till. Then there was the drinking, coming in still drunk, coming in late or not coming in at all. I liked her mother, so I tried to help the girl." He shook his head. "Finally, I had to let her go, you understand."

Frankie blinked. He couldn't be talking about the same Naomi Hank had been involved with. "We're talking about Naomi Hill, the one who—"

"Jumped off the cliff and killed herself. Yes."

Stealing? Drinking? Partying? Blowing off work? She tried to figure out how that went with the image Hank had painted of Naomi, but the two didn't fit.

A thought struck her. "She wasn't doing all this alone, right? There had to be someone she hung out with that might be able to give me some insight into her character."

He nodded. "Tamara Baker."

"Is she still around?"

"She works at the Silver Spur Bar." She didn't have to ask him what he thought of Tamara. He glanced at the clock on the wall. "She should be coming to work about now. If she is able to." He shook his head. "I hope this has helped you. I find it most disturbing to revisit it."

"You have been a great help, thank you." She got to her feet, feeling unsteady from the shock of what she'd learned. Sweet, timid little Naomi. Frankie couldn't wait to talk to her friend Tamara.

WHEN HUD CAME home for lunch, as he always did, Dana had sandwiches made and a fresh pot of coffee ready. She hadn't planned to say anything until he'd finished eating.

"What is it?" her husband demanded. "You look as if you're about to pop. Spit it out."

She hurriedly sat down with him and took half of a sandwich onto her plate. Broaching this subject was difficult. They'd discussed Hank on occasion but it never ended well. Sometimes her husband could be so mule-headed stubborn.

"It's Hank."

"Of course it is," Hud said with a curse.

"Something's wrong."

Her husband shook his head as he took a bite of his lunch, clearly just wanting to eat and get out of there.

"This relationship with Frankie, it just doesn't feel...real."

"You have talked about nothing else but your hopes and prayers for Hank to move on, get over Naomi, make a life for himself. Now that he's doing it—"

"I don't believe he's doing it. Maybe coming back here was the worst thing he could do. I can tell it's putting a strain on him and Frankie. Earlier, I saw them… They aren't as loving toward each other as they should be."

Hud groaned as he finished his sandwich and reached for a cookie, which he dunked angrily into his coffee mug. "What would you like *me* to do about it?"

"Why is it we can't talk about Hank without you getting angry?" she demanded. They hardly ever argued, but when it came to the kids, she was like a mama bear, even with Hud. "I want to know more about Frankie." She said the words that had been rolling around in her mind since she'd first met the woman.

"You don't like her."

"No, I do. That's the problem. She seems so right for Hank."

Hud raked a hand through his hair before settling his gaze on her. "What am I missing here?"

"That's just it. I like her so much, I have to be sure this isn't— I mean, that she's not— Can't you just do some checking on her to relieve my mind so I can—"

"No." He stood up so abruptly that the dishes on the table rattled, startling her. "Absolutely not. Have you forgotten that the trouble began between my son and me when I did a background check on Naomi?"

"Because he was so in love with her. It was his first real crush. I asked you to make sure that she was all right for him because he seemed blind to her…"

"Blind to the fact that she didn't want what he wanted more than anything? That she would never have been happy with Hank if he settled here? She wanted marriage so badly that it was all she talked about. That she was pressuring our son and I could see that he felt backed against a wall?" Hud demanded. "Yes. Those were all good reasons. Along with the fact that I sensed a weakness in her. A fragility…"

"You questioned her mental stability, not to mention she'd been arrested for shoplifting."

He nodded, looking sick. "Something I never told our son. As it turned out, maybe I should have. I was right about her, which gives me no satisfaction." He raised his head to meet her gaze. His eyes shone. "I lost my son. I'm not sure I will get him back because of everything that happened. I can't make that mistake again." He reached for his Stetson on the wall hook where he put it each time he entered the kitchen. "Thank you for lunch." With that, he left.

Dana looked after him, fighting tears. She couldn't help the knot of fear inside her. Something was wrong, but she had no idea what to do about it.

TAMARA BAKER WAS indeed behind the bar at the Silver Spur. The place was empty, a janitor was just finishing up in the restroom, and the smell of industrial-strength cleanser permeated the air.

"Tamara Baker?" Frankie asked as she took a barstool.

"Who wants to know?" asked the brunette behind the bar. She had a smoker's rough voice and a hard-lived face that belied her real age. Frankie estimated she was in her midthirties, definitely older than Naomi.

"You knew Naomi Hill."

Tamara's eyes narrowed to slits. "You a reporter?"

Frankie laughed. "Not hardly. I heard that you and Naomi used to party together."

"That's no secret." That was what she thought. "But if you aren't with the press, then—"

Frankie gave her the same story she had Roy, only Tamara wasn't quite as gullible. When Frankie flashed her credentials, the bartender grabbed them, taking them over into the light from the back bar to study them.

"You're a PI? No kidding?"

"No kidding. I was hoping you could tell me about Naomi. Other people I've spoken with have painted a completely different picture of her compared to the stories I've heard about the two of you." She was exaggerating, but the fib worked.

Tamara laughed. "Want something to drink?" she asked as she poured herself one.

"I'd take a cola."

"I knew a different side of Naomi," the woman said after taking a pull of her drink. "She let her freak flag fly when she was with me."

"How did you two meet?"

"At the grocery store. She helped me out sometimes when I didn't have enough money to feed my kids." Tamara shrugged. "I tried to pay her back by showing her a good time here at the bar."

Frankie understood perfectly. Naomi would steal out of the till at the grocery store for Tamara, and Tamara would ply her with free drinks here at the bar. "What about men?"

"*Men?* What about them?"

"Did this wild side of her also include men?"

Tamara finished her drink and washed out

the glass. "Naomi wasn't interested. She had this rancher she said she was going to marry. She flirted a little, but she was saving herself for marriage. She had this idea that once she was married, everything would come up roses." The bartender laughed.

"You doubted it?"

"I've seen women come through here thinking that marriage was going to cure whatever ailed them," Tamara said. "I've been there. What about you?" she asked, glancing at Frankie's left hand. "You married?"

She shook her head. "You must have been surprised when you heard that Naomi dove off the cliff and killed herself."

The woman snorted. "I figured it was just a matter of time. She was living a double life. It was bound to catch up with her."

"You mean between the bar and the cowboy?"

Tamara looked away for a moment as if she thought someone might be listening. "Naomi had a lot more going on than anyone knew."

"Such as?"

The front door opened, sending a shaft of bright summer sun streaming across the floor like a laser in their direction. A man entered, the door closing behind him, pitching them back into cool darkness.

"Hey, Darrel," she called to the man as he limped to the bar. "What ya havin'?" The bartender got a beer for the man and hung around talking to him quietly for a few minutes.

Frankie saw the man glance in her direction. He was about her age with sandy-blond hair, not bad-looking, but there was something about him that made her look away. He seemed to be suddenly focusing on her a little too intensely. She wondered what Tamara had told him about her.

When the bartender came back down the bar, Frankie asked, "You didn't happen to see Naomi that night, the night she died, did you?"

"Me?" She shook her head. "I was working until closing. It's my usual shift. You can ask anyone."

Frankie noticed that the woman now seemed nervous and kept glancing down the bar at the man she'd called Darrel.

As she straightened the shirt she was wearing, Tamara asked, "Can I get you anything else?" She didn't sound all that enthusiastic about it.

"You said Naomi was into other things. Like what?"

"I was just shooting my mouth off. You can't pay any attention to me. If I can't get you anything else, I really need to do some stocking up." She tilted her head toward the man at the end of the bar. She lowered her voice. "You know, want to look good in front of the customers."

"Sure." She could tell that was all she was going to get out of Tamara. But she wondered what it was about the man at the end of the bar that made her nervous.

As she left, she found herself still trying to piece together what she'd learned about the woman known as Naomi Hill. The pieces didn't fit. She tried to imagine what Naomi could have been involved in that would get her murdered—if that had been the case.

More and more, though, Frankie believed that the woman had come unhinged when she'd seen her planned life with Hank crumbling, and it had driven her to do the one thing that terrified her more than her so-called double life.

HANK KNEW HE couldn't put it off any longer. He swung by his father's office, knowing the man was a creature of habit. Marshal Hudson Savage went home every day for lunch. And every day, his wife would have a meal ready. Hank used to find it sweet. Then his father went back to his office. If nothing was happening, he would do paperwork for an hour or so before he would go out on patrol.

He found his father sitting behind his desk. The marshal looked up in surprise to see Hank standing in the doorway. "Come on in," he said, as if he knew this wasn't a personal visit. "Close the door."

Hank did just that, but he didn't take the chair his father offered him. "I want a copy of Naomi's file." Hud started to shake his head. "Don't tell me I can't have it. She'd dead. The case is closed. Pretend I'm a reporter and give me a copy."

His father sighed as he leaned back in his chair, gazing at him with an intensity that used to scare him when he was a boy and in trouble. "Your mother and I had hoped—"

"I know what you'd hoped," he interrupted. "Don't read too much into my wanting a copy of the file."

"What am I supposed not to read into it? That you still haven't moved on?"

Hank said nothing.

"What's the deal with you and Frankie?" the marshal asked, no longer sounding like his father. "Are you in love with her?"

"Seriously? Mother put you up to this?"

"We're concerned."

Hank laughed. "Just like you were concerned when I was in love with Naomi."

"Are you in love with Frankie?"

"Who wouldn't be? She's a beautiful, smart, talented woman. Now, if we're through with the interrogation, I still want that file. Let's say I need it to get closure."

"Is that what it is?"

He gave his father an impatient look.

The marshal leaned forward, picked up a manila envelope from his desk and held it out to him.

Hank stared at it without taking the envelope from him for a moment. "What is this?"

"A copy of Naomi's file."

"How—"

"How did I know that you would be asking for it?" His father asked the question for him as he cocked his head. Hank noticed his father's hair more graying than he remembered. "Maybe I know you better than you think."

Hank took the envelope from him. "Is everything in here?"

"Everything, including my notes. Will there be anything else?"

He shook his head, feeling as if there was something more he should say. "Thank you."

His father gave him a nod. His desk phone rang.

Hank opened the door, looking back as his

father picked up the phone and said, "Marshal Savage." He let the door close behind him and left.

Chapter Ten

J.J. went by Frankie's apartment and banged on the door until the neighbor opened a window and yelled out.

"I'm going to call the cops."

"Call the cops. Where's Frankie?"

"The woman who lives in that apartment? She packed up and left with some man a few days ago."

"What?" He described Frankie to the man since it was clear the fool didn't know what he was talking about.

"That's her," the man said. "I know my own neighbor. She left with a cowboy—that's all I can tell you. She's not home, so please let me get some sleep."

He thought he might lose his mind. Where could she have gone? He'd been by her office. It was locked up tight. He told himself she was on a case. But why wouldn't she answer her phone? Why wouldn't she call him back? She knew what a mistake that would be once he got his hands on her.

He'd called her number, left more messages, and still she hadn't gotten back to him. What if she'd left for good?

She wouldn't do that. She was just trying to teach him a lesson, playing hard to get. Once he saw her again, he'd teach *her* a lesson she wouldn't soon forget. No one pulled this kind of crap on him. Especially some woman.

He knew there was only one thing to do. Track her down and make her pay.

After all, he had the resources. He just hadn't wanted to use them. He'd hoped that Frankie would have come to her senses and realized she couldn't get away from him. But she had.

And now he was going after her.

FRANKIE FOUND HANK poring over papers on the small table in their cabin.

Hank looked up, surprised as she came in the door, as if he'd forgotten all about her. "Where have *you* been?"

"I've been working. You all right?"

He nodded. "I stopped by the marshal's office and got a copy of Naomi's file."

"Your dad gave it to you?" She couldn't help being surprised.

"He'd already made a copy for me." He grunted. "He says he knows me better than I think he does. You're probably right about them seeing through us. Mom said you took one of the pickups into town. I'm sorry I didn't think to give you keys for a vehicle."

"It was fine," she said, pulling out a chair at the table and sitting down. "I had coffee and cookies with your mother before I left."

He raised a brow. "How did that go?"

"She quizzed me about us, about me. She wanted to know how we met. We should have come up with something beforehand. I had to wing it." She told him the story she'd given to his mother.

Hank nodded. "Sorry about that, but it sounds like you covered it."

"We had a nice visit. I don't like lying to her, though. She's going to be hurt."

"I know." He got to his feet. "You hungry? I haven't had lunch."

"Me either."

"I know a place up the canyon, the Corral. They used to make great burgers. Want to give it a try?"

She smiled as her stomach rumbled loudly.

It was one of those beautiful summer days. Frankie breathed it in as Hank drove them through the canyon. Sunlight glimmered off the pines and the clear green of the river as the road and river wound together through cliffs and meadows.

Frankie sat back and enjoyed the ride. She'd decided she would tell Hank later what she'd learned so as not to spoil his lunch. It could wait, and right now she was enjoying just the two of them on this amazing day. Even Hank seemed more relaxed than she'd seen him. He turned on the radio, and as a country song came on from a local station, they both burst into song. Frankie had grown up on the old country classics, so she knew all the words.

They laughed as the song ended and fell into a companionable silence as the news came on and Hank turned off the radio.

"You said you were working while I was gone—"

"We can talk about it later."

He shot her a look before going back to his driving, as if he knew it wasn't going to be good news. Not far up the road he turned into the Corral. The place had originally been built in 1947. It had changed from when Hank was a boy, but it still served great burgers and fries. Now you could also get buffalo as well as beef and sweet potato fries or regular. The booths had been replaced with log furniture and yet he still felt as at home here as he had as a boy when his grandfather used to play guitar in a band here.

After they ordered, Hank said, "I like your hair." He reached over and caught a long lock between his thumb and finger. "Do you ever wear it down?"

She eyed him suspiciously.

"What? I can't compliment you? You said we needed to act like lovers."

"Lovers?" She broke into a smile. "Something happen I don't know about?"

He let go of her hair and glanced toward the bar. "Before I went down to my father's office for a copy of Naomi's file, I stopped by the river again where she died. There was someone else there. I heard them behind me and when I turned around they ran. I caught only a glimpse of fabric through the trees and then I heard a car engine start up and the vehicle leave."

FRANKIE COULD SEE that the incident had spooked him. She wasn't sure why, though. Nothing about it sounded sinister. "Who do you think it was?"

He shook his head. "I thought I caught a glimpse of Naomi up on the ledge, wearing this pale yellow dress she loved."

"Was anyone up on the ledge?"

He shook his head. "But there was someone behind me. Someone wearing a light-colored garment running through the trees."

"You thought it was Naomi?"

"Naomi is dead. She can't step on a twig and break it directly behind me and startle me." He picked up his napkin and rearranged his silverware. "I'm not losing it."

"I know you're not. You saw someone. But that doesn't mean it had anything to do with Naomi. Unless you think you were followed."

He shook his head. "Why would someone follow me?"

She shrugged. Clearly neither of them knew. He realized that she was right. It was just someone who was looking for a spot on the river. He'd probably startled them more than they had him.

"But then again," Frankie said, "if you're right and Naomi was murdered, then her murderer is still out there."

"If you're trying to scare me—"

"What you have to figure out is why anyone would want to kill Naomi in the first place. I have some thoughts that I'll share on the way back to the ranch. But in the meantime—"

"Just a minute. You learned something?"

Fortunately, their burgers and fries came just then. They'd both gone for beef, regular fries and colas. Hank looked down at the food, then at her. She picked up a fry and dragged it through a squirt of ketchup she'd poured onto her plate before taking a bite.

"I can't remember the last time I had a burger and fries," she said with enthusiasm. Picking up the burger, she took a juicy hot bite and made a *hmmm* sound that had him smiling.

He could see that she didn't want to talk about what she'd found out. Not now. He decided to let it go until after their lunch because it was a beautiful day and he was sitting here with a beautiful woman. "Did I just see you put mayo on your burger?"

"You have a problem with that?" she joked.

He reached for the side of mayo she'd ordered. "Not if you share. I guess it's just one more thing we have in common."

"We have something in common?"

Hank met her gaze. "Maybe more than you realize." He took a bite of his burger and they ate as if it might be their last meal.

HANK COULDN'T REMEMBER the last time he'd enjoyed a meal more—or his dining companion. Frankie was funnier than he'd expected her to be. The more time he spent around her, the more he liked her. She'd definitely been the right choice when he'd gone looking for a private investigator.

He'd asked around and was told he couldn't beat Frankie Brewster. At that point, he'd thought Frankie was male. It wasn't until he saw her that he knew how to come back to the ranch without drawing attention to his reason for returning. So far, it seemed to be working, even if his parents were suspicious of their relationship. Let them worry about that instead of his real reason for bringing her home.

"Okay, let's hear it," he said as they left the Corral and headed the five miles back toward Big Sky and the ranch.

She started to say something when she glanced in her side mirror. "Do you know the driver of that truck behind us?"

He glanced in his rearview mirror and saw a large gold older-model truck behind them. As he watched, he saw that the truck was gaining speed on them. "No, why?"

"I saw it behind us earlier on the way to the Corral."

"You think whoever is driving it is following us?" The idea sounded ludicrous until he reminded himself of the person he'd seen by the river earlier—and the reason he was home. She was right. If Naomi had been murdered, then her killer was still out there.

Looking in the rearview again, he saw that the truck was coming up way too fast. The canyon road was winding with tight curves and few straightaways, and yet the driver of the truck acted as if he planned to pass—and soon—given the speed he was traveling.

"Hank, I have a bad feeling," Frankie said as the driver of the truck closed the distance.

He had the same bad feeling. Earlier there'd been more traffic, especially close to Big Sky, but other than a few semis passing by, they seemed to be the only two vehicles on this stretch of the highway right now.

Hank looked for a place to pull off and let the truck pass. Maybe it was a driver who didn't know this canyon and how dangerous it could be. Or maybe— The front of the truck filled his rearview mirror.

"He's going to ram us," he cried. "Brace yourself."

The driver of the truck slammed into the back of them. Hank fought to keep the pickup on the road. This section of highway was bordered on one side by cliffs and the river on the other. Fortunately, there was a guardrail along the river, but up ahead there was a spot where the guardrail was broken apart from a previous accident and hadn't been replaced yet.

All thoughts of the driver of the truck behind them being new to the area dissolved. Whoever was at that wheel knew exactly what he was doing. Hank knew going faster wasn't going to help. He couldn't outrun the truck.

"He's going to try to knock us into the river at this next curve," he told Frankie as the bumper of the truck banged into them again and he had to fight the wheel to keep from wrecking. "There is nothing I can do, so I have a bad feeling we will be swimming soon."

As he came around the curve, the trucker did exactly what he'd anticipated he would do. Hank tried to stay on the highway, but the truck was too large, the driver going too fast. The large truck smashed into the side of his pickup, forcing them off the road. Fortunately, Hank saw that the riverbank wasn't steep. Rather than let the trucker roll the pickup off into the river, he turned the wheel sharply toward the water and yelled, "Hang on!" and hoped for the best as the pickup left the highway and plunged into the Gallatin River.

Chapter Eleven

"I was just at the grocery store," Dana said without preamble when her husband answered his phone at the marshal's office. "I overheard the manager talking to one of his employees about Naomi."

"Dana, I'm right in the middle of—"

"Roy said that a woman named Francesca Brewster with some insurance company had come in and was asking questions about Naomi and her death. Why would Frankie be asking about Naomi's death?"

"Maybe she's curious," her husband said after a moment. "After all, Naomi was Hank's former girlfriend. Frankie probably wants to know what happened to her and I doubt Hank is very forthcoming. Hell, he still thinks she was murdered."

"I'm worried. You know how I felt about Naomi and I'm afraid Hank did too. Now it's like he doesn't trust me. I have no idea how he feels about Frankie."

"He brought her home with him. That should tell you something."

"It would if they were getting along. Stacy said they aren't sleeping in the same bed and earlier I saw them having another argument. If she's asking people questions about Naomi—"

"I think you're making too much out of this."

"We don't know anything about her."

"Dana—"

"He's our son, Hud. I don't want to see him make a terrible—"

"There is nothing we can do about it. If either of us says anything…" He swore. "Honey, we have to let him make his own mistakes. We both tried to warn him about Naomi and look where that left us."

"It's just that I don't think he can take another woman breaking his heart." She hated how close to tears she sounded.

"He's a grown man. He can take care of himself. Give him a little credit. Maybe Frankie is exactly what he needs."

IT HAPPENED SO FAST, Frankie didn't have time to react. One minute they were on the highway, the next in the river. The pickup plunged into the water, the front smashing into the rocks. Water rushed around them and began to come in through the cracks, building up quickly at her side window.

"We have to get out of here," Hank yelled over the roar of the river and the sound of water as it began to fill the cab.

She saw him try to open his door and fail against the weight of water. Her door was facing upstream, so she knew there was no opening it. She unhooked her seat belt, only then aware of her deflated airbag in her lap. Water was rising quickly. Hank was right. They had to brave the river because if they stayed in the pickup much longer—

Next to her, Hank had unsnapped his seat belt and was trying to get his side window to slide down, but it didn't appear to be working. He moved over and leaned back against her. "Get ready," he said. "Once I kick out the window…" He didn't need to tell her what would happen. She could see the water rushing over the cab of the pickup and forming an eddy on his side of the truck.

Hank reared back and kicked. The glass turned into a white spiderweb. He kicked again and the window disappeared out into the river. Cold water rushed in. Hank grabbed her hand. "Hang on," he said as the cab filled faster.

She held on as if her life depended on it. It did. For a moment, the force of the water rushing in wouldn't let them escape. But Hank kicked off the side of the pickup, dragging her with him. For a few moments, which felt like an eternity, she saw and felt nothing but water all around her. Her chest ached from holding her breath. She needed air, would have done anything for one small intake of oxygen. Hank never let go of her hand, or her his, even as the river tried to pull them apart.

And then, gloriously, they surfaced, and she gasped for breath. Nothing had ever felt so good as she took air into her lungs. As Hank pulled her toward shore, she looked back, surprised by how far downriver they'd surfaced. The truck cab was completely submerged in the water. She coughed and gasped for air as she stumbled up onto the rocks.

Hank pulled her to him, rubbing her arms as if to take away the chill. She hadn't realized how hard she was trembling until his strong body wrapped around her. She leaned into him, taking comfort in his warmth as what had just happened finally hit her. Someone had tried to kill them—and she'd lost her purse as well as her gun.

On the highway, vehicles had stopped. People were calling to them. Someone said they'd phoned for help and that the marshal was on his way.

DRENCHED TO THE skin and still shivering from the cold water and the close call, Hank climbed into the back of his father's patrol SUV with Frankie. His father had given them blankets, which they'd wrapped up in. Still he put his arm around her, holding her close to share his body heat. He still couldn't believe what had happened and was just thankful they were both alive.

He'd gotten her into this. So of course he felt responsible for her. But he knew it was more than that as he pulled her closer. He wasn't sure when it had happened but they felt like friends. Almost dying did that to a person, he thought.

He became aware of how her wet clothes clung to her, revealing curves he'd always known were there but hadn't seen before. The fact that he could think about that now told him that he was definitely alive—and typically male.

"Why would someone want to force you off the road?" his father asked after he'd told him what had happened.

He heard the disbelief in his father's tone. He'd been here before. Hud hadn't believed that Naomi was murdered. He didn't believe that someone had just tried to kill them. "Believe whatever you like," he snapped. "But this was no accident. The truck crashed into us twice before it forced me off the road. It wasn't a case of road rage. Frankie had seen it behind us on the way to the Corral. The driver must have followed us and waited until we came out."

"Okay, son. I've called for a wrecker. I'll have your truck taken to the lab. Hopefully there will be some paint from the other truck on it that will help us track down the make and model, along with the description you've already given me of the driver. Even if the driver wasn't trying to kill the two of you, he left the scene of an accident. I've put a BOLO out. Later, after the two of you get a shower and warm clothes on, I'll take your statements."

Hank rested his head on the top of Frankie's as she leaned into his chest and tried not to let his father get to him. The man always had to be Marshal Hudson Savage, all business. The show-me-the-evidence lawman. Just for once, Hank would have liked him to believe his own son.

He drew Frankie closer and closed his eyes,

just thankful to be alive. Thankful he hadn't gotten her killed. And more aware than ever of the woman in his arms.

FRANKIE FELT AS if she was in shock. After they were dropped off at their cabin, Hank led her into the bathroom and turned on the shower. *It's probably hypothermia*, she thought, since she'd felt fine in Hank's arms, but the moment he'd let her go, she'd begun to shake again.

The mirror in the bathroom quickly steamed over. "Get in with your clothes on." She looked at him as if he'd lost his mind. "Seriously," he said and, opening the glass shower door, pushed her toward the warm water streaming down from the showerhead. "Just toss your wet clothes on the floor of the shower. I'll take care of them later. I'll use the other shower. You need to get warm and dry as quickly as possible. Trust me."

Trust him? She looked into his handsome face and had to smile. Surprising herself, she did as he suggested and stepped into the walk-in shower, clothes and all. She did trust him. More than he knew. The warm water felt so good as it soaked her clothing and took away the cold. With trembling fingers, she began to peel off the wet garments to let the warm water get to her bare skin.

She felt something heavy in her jeans pocket. Her cell phone. She pulled it out and reached out to lay it next to the sink. At least she wouldn't have to worry about getting any more calls she didn't want to take since she could see that the screen was fogged over, the phone no doubt dead.

Worse, earlier, she'd put her gun into her purse. She could only hope that her purse had stayed in the pickup. Otherwise, it had washed downriver.

A shiver moved through her and she stepped back into the shower. But she knew that it would take more than warm water to stop her from shaking. Someone had tried to kill them. She thought about the truck that had forced them off the highway and into the river. She'd only glimpsed the driver. A man. A large angry man.

It wasn't him, she told herself. It couldn't have been. Where would he have gotten a truck like that and how would he—

Unless he had somehow tracked her to Big Sky. She glanced at her phone and felt her heart drop. Tracking her phone would have been child's play for anyone who knew how. Especially for a cop.

She leaned against the shower wall, suddenly weak with fear. The last thing she wanted was her past catching up with her here. She told herself that she was only running scared. He hadn't found her. The man in the truck hadn't been him. All of this was about Naomi—not about her.

Refusing to give in to her fears that she might have been responsible for almost getting Hank killed, she concentrated on the feel of the warm water cascading down her body. As she turned her face up to the spray, she assured herself that she was fine. Hank was fine. Better than fine. She thought of how he'd held on to her until they were both safe on shore and then hugged her in his arms, sharing his warmth, protecting her, taking care of her even when he had to be as cold as she was.

She felt her nipples pucker to aching tips at the memory of his hard body against hers. It had been so long since she'd felt desire for a man. It spiked through her, turning her molten at her center at just the thought of Hank in the other shower, warm water running down his naked body.

Frankie shut off the water and, stepping over her wet clothes, reached for a towel. Hank was her employer. Nothing more. She was reacting to him like this only because they'd just shared a near-death experience.

But even as she thought it, Frankie knew

it was much more than that. She'd never met anyone like Hank. His capacity to love astounded her. Look how he'd mourned Naomi's death for three long years and still refused to give up on finding out the truth. Frankie couldn't imagine a man loving her like that.

She toweled herself dry and pulled on the robe she saw that Hank had left for her. After drawing it around her, she pulled up the collar and smelled the freshly washed scent. Hugging herself, she realized she was crying softly. She'd never been so happy to be alive.

Frankie quickly wiped her tears and busied herself wringing out her clothes and hanging them in the shower to dry. Then, bracing herself, she tied the robe tightly around her and stepped out of the bathroom.

HUD RETURNED TO his office. He quickly checked to make sure that a deputy and a highway patrol officer were taking care of traffic while the wrecker retrieved Hank's pickup from the river.

He realized he was still shaken. He didn't want to believe that the driver of the truck who'd run them off the road had been trying to kill them. But the driver had forced them off the road where the guardrail was missing—as if he knew exactly where to dump them into the river. That made the driver a local and that was what worried Hud.

Hank believed this had something to do with Naomi's death. But Hud had seen Frankie's face in the rearview mirror. She'd just been through a terrifying experience, no doubt about it. Yet he'd seen a fear in her eyes long after she'd been safe and warm in the back of his patrol SUV.

Swearing under his breath, he turned on his computer, his fingers hovering over the keys for a moment as he considered what he was about to do. He ticked off the reasons he had to do this. Hank's unexpected return. His son bringing a woman home after three years. Francesca "Frankie" Brewster, someone they'd never heard about before. The two were allegedly a couple, but their behavior was in question by Dana, who was good at these things. Add to that, Frankie had been asking around about Naomi's death. Throw in the "accident" that ended up with them in the river and what did it give you?

With a curse, he put his fingertips on the computer keys and typed Francesca "Frankie" Brewster, Lost Creek, Idaho.

What popped up on the screen made him release the breath he'd been holding. He sat back, staring at the screen. What the hell? Frankie Brewster Investigations?

It took him only another minute to find out that she was a licensed private investigator in the state of Idaho and had been in business for four years. Her name came up in articles in the local paper. She'd actually solved a few cases that had made the news.

He sat back again, berating himself for looking and, at the same time, wondering what he was going to do now with the information. Just because she was a PI didn't mean that she and Hank weren't really a couple. In fact, Hud thought that might be what attracted his son to her to begin with. So why make waves?

If he said anything to Hank, his son would be furious. He would know that his father did it again, checked up on Frankie—just as he had with Naomi. Only with Frankie there was no sign that she'd ever been arrested or put under mental evaluation, at least.

"That's a plus," he said to himself and turned off the computer to rub the back of his neck and mentally kick himself. "Frankie's investigating Naomi's death," he said to himself, realizing that was what was going on. His son thought he could pull a fast one, bring Frankie home, pretend to be an item, and all the time the two were digging into Naomi's death.

He swore under his breath. Was it possible that someone was getting nervous? Was that why that truck had forced them off the road? To warn them to stop? But if that was the case...

Hud picked up the phone and called the lab. "I want information on the vehicle that forced that pickup off the road ASAP. Call me at home when you get it."

In all his years in law enforcement, he'd never felt this unsettled. What if Hank had been right all along and Naomi had been murdered? Enter Frankie, and the next thing he knew, his son and the PI were run off the highway and into the river. A little too coincidental to suit him.

With a sigh, he knew what he had to do. He had to stop them from investigating even if it meant making his son mad at him again. Hank had to let him look into it. Even as he thought it, Hud knew hell would freeze over before his son would trust him to do that. There would be no stopping Frankie and Hank if they were doing what he suspected they were.

He thought of all the mistakes he'd made with his oldest son. As he got to his feet, he just prayed that he wasn't about to make an even bigger one. But he had to stop the two of them before they ended up dead.

HANK CAME OUT of the bathroom only moments after Frankie. He'd stood under the warm spray for a long time. His emotions were all over the place. The trucker running them off the road proved what he'd been saying all along, didn't it?

So why didn't he feel more satisfaction? He'd been right. But as he stood letting the water cascade over his body, all he'd been able to think about was Frankie. He kept picturing her soaking wet, her clothes clinging to every curve. The memory had him aching.

He had turned the shower to cold and tried to get a handle on his feelings. Shivering again, he'd turned off the shower and had stood for a moment, still flooded with a desire like none he'd ever felt. He'd loved Naomi but she hadn't stirred this kind of passion in him. Was that another reason he hadn't wanted to rush into marriage?

Shaking his head, he'd stepped out of the shower and grabbed a towel to roughly dry himself off. He didn't want to be feeling these yearnings toward Frankie, not when he'd come home to set things right with Naomi. He told himself that he would keep her at a distance.

But try as he might, he still felt an aching need at even the memory of her in his arms in the back of the patrol SUV.

He'd hung up his wet clothes and pulled on one of the guest robes that his mother supplied to the cabins. He promised himself that he would keep his mind on the investigation. If he was right, then they had rattled Naomi's killer. They were getting close. Maybe too close, he'd thought as he'd stepped out of the bedroom.

At the sight of Frankie standing there, his bare feet faltered on the wood floor. Her long, dark hair was down, hanging below her shoulders to the tips of her breasts beneath the robe. Her face was flushed, as was her neck and throat. Water droplets still clung to her eyelashes, making her eyes appear even larger, the violet a darker purple.

She looked stunning. When their gazes met, he saw a need in her that matched his own and felt all his resolve to keep her at arm's length evaporate before his eyes. He closed the distance between them without a word, without a thought. She didn't move, her gaze locked with his, a vein in her slim neck throbbing as he approached.

He took a lock of her long hair in his fingers. It felt silken even wet. She still hadn't moved. Still hadn't broken eye contact. His heart pounded as he brushed her hair back on one side before leaning in to kiss that spot on her neck where her blood pulsed. The throbbing beat quickened beneath his lips and it was as if he could feel his own heart drumming wildly to the same beat.

It had been so long since he'd felt like this. As his lips traveled down her neck into the hollow at her shoulder, she leaned back, giving him access. He heard her sharp intake of breath as he stroked her tender flesh with the tip of his tongue. From the hollow at her shoulder, it would have been too easy to dip down to the opening of her robe and swell of her breasts he could see rising and falling with each of her breaths.

He lifted his head again to look into her eyes before he cupped the back of her neck and drew her into a kiss, dragging her body against his. Desire raced along his veins to the riotous pounding of his heart. She looped her arms around his neck as he deepened the kiss and pulled her even closer until their bodies were molded together, almost as one. He could feel her breasts straining against the robe. He wanted desperately to lay open her robe and press his skin to hers. He wanted her naked body beneath his more than he wanted his next breath.

Reaching down, he pulled the sash of her robe. It fell away. He untied his own. As their robes opened, he pushed the fabric aside. He heard a gasp escape her lips as their warm, naked bodies came together. He felt her hard nipples press against his chest. Desire shot through him.

The knock at the door startled them both. "Hank? Frankie? I need to talk to you." Another knock and then the knob turned slowly.

They burst apart, both frantically retying their robes as the marshal stuck his head in the door. "Sorry. I…" He started to close the door.

"It's all right," Hank said. His voice sounded hoarse with emotion and need even to his ears. He shot a look at Frankie and saw that she was as shaken as he was. If only he had thought to lock the door. If only his father had picked any time but now to stop by.

And yet, now that he'd cooled down some, he knew it was for the best. He had enough problems without jumping into bed with Frankie—as much as he would have loved to do just that. But life was complicated enough as it was. A part of him was still in love with Naomi. He wasn't sure he'd ever get over her—and he had a feeling that Frankie knew that.

"Did you find out something about the truck that ran us off the road?" Frankie asked, her voice breaking.

They shared a look. Both of them struggling not to laugh at the irony of the situation. He wondered if she felt as disappointed as he did—and maybe just as relieved. Their relationship was complicated enough without this. And, he reminded himself, there was that man who kept calling her, the one Frankie didn't want to talk to. The one he suspected was her lover, past or present. Whoever the man was, Frankie hadn't dealt with him, he thought as his father stepped into the cabin, Stetson in hand and a sheepish, amused and yet curious look on his face.

HUD LOOKED FROM his son to Frankie. Both were flushed and not just from their showers. He hadn't known what he was going to say, but after walking in on what he'd just seen, he surprised himself.

"I've decided to reopen Naomi's case," he said as the two hurriedly moved away from each other like teenagers caught necking on the couch. Dana had thought they weren't lovers. If he hadn't come along when he did, they would have been. Maybe his wife was wrong about the two of them. Maybe he was too.

"Why would you reopen the case?" Hank asked as Frankie straightened her robe.

"I'm going to get dressed," she said. "If you'll excuse me." She hurried off toward the bedroom.

"I'm sorry," Hud said. "Clearly I interrupted something."

His son waved a hand through the air. "I thought you didn't believe that Naomi was murdered?"

"I'm still not sure I do. But after what happened today, I want to take another look."

Hank shook his head, mumbling under his breath as he turned toward the kitchen. "I'm going to get dressed and have a beer. You want one?"

He glanced at his watch. He was off the clock. Normally he would pass because he wasn't in the habit of drinking before dinner, but today he'd make an exception. "I would love one." That apparently had taken Hank by surprise, because he felt his son studying him as Hank returned in jeans and a Western shirt with two bottles of beer.

As Hank handed him one and twisted off the top on his own, he said, "Thank Mom for stocking our refrigerator."

"You know your mother. She wanted you and Frankie to be...comfortable up here." Earlier, he'd come up to the cabin, planning to bust them, exposing Frankie as a PI and their relationship as a fraud. But seeing them together, he'd changed his mind and was glad of it. He could eat a little crow with his son.

Anyway, what would it hurt to reopen the case unofficially? He still had misgivings about Hank's accident earlier today. Maybe all it had been was road rage. Either way, he was determined to track down the truck— and driver.

Frankie came out of the bedroom dressed in a baggy shirt and jeans, her feet still bare. Without asking her, Hank handed her his untouched beer and went into the kitchen to get another one.

Hud stood for a moment, he and Frankie somewhat uneasy in each other's presence. He was sure that his son had given the PI an earful about him. He'd lost Hank's respect because of Naomi's case. He'd thought he wouldn't get another chance to redeem himself. Maybe this would be it.

Hud took a chair while Frankie curled up on the couch, leaving the chair opposite him open. Hank, though, appeared too restless or stubborn to sit. He stood sipping his beer.

"Any word on the truck that put us in the river?" Frankie asked into the dead silence that followed.

"Not yet. I've asked that it be moved to priority one," he said. "I also have law enforcement in the canyon watching for the truck. It will turn up." He sounded more confident than he felt. He needed that truck and its driver. He needed to find out what had happened earlier and why—and not just to show his son that he knew what he was doing. If Hank was right and the driver of that truck was somehow connected to Naomi's death…well, then he needed to find Naomi's killer—before his son and Frankie did.

"If I was wrong, I'll make it right," he told his son, who nodded, though grudgingly. As he finished his beer, his cell phone rang. "That will be your mother. Don't tell her about this," he said, holding up his empty bottle. "We'll both be in trouble," he joked, then sobered. "Dinner isn't for a while. But I also would play down what happened earlier in the river during the meal. You know your mother."

Hank smiled. "I certainly do." Hud saw him glance at Frankie. A look passed between them, one he couldn't read, but he could feel the heat of it. He really wished his timing had been better earlier.

FRANKIE WAS STILL shaken from those moments with Hank before the marshal had arrived. She'd come so close to opening herself up to him, to baring not just her naked body, but her soul. She couldn't let that happen again. She reminded herself that their relationship was fake. He was her employer. He was still in love with the memory of Naomi.

That last part especially, she couldn't let herself forget. Not to mention the fact that she had her own baggage he knew nothing about. With luck, he never would. Once she was finished with this job, she would return to Idaho. Who knew what Hank would do.

Clearly, he loved the ranch and wanted to be part of the family's ranching operation. Would what they discovered free him from the past? Free him from Naomi enough that he could return?

"We have time for a horseback ride," Hank said out of the blue as the marshal left. "It's time you saw the ranch. You do ride, don't you?"

"I grew up in Montana before I moved to Idaho," she said. "It's been years since I've ridden, but I do know the front of the horse from the back."

"Good enough," Hank said. "Come on."

Frankie got the feeling that he didn't want

to be alone with her in their cabin for fear of what would happen between them. She felt relieved but also a little disappointed, which made her angry with herself. Had she learned nothing when it came to men?

They walked down to the barn, where Hank saddled them a couple of horses. She stood in the sunlight that hung over Lone Mountain and watched him. She liked the way he used his hands and how gentle he was with the horses. There were many sides to this handsome cowboy, she thought as he patted her horse's neck and said, "Buttercup, you be nice to Frankie, now."

He handed her the reins. "Buttercup said she'll be nice. You need to do the same. No cursing her if she tries to brush you off under a pine tree." He turned to take the reins of the other horse.

"Wait," Frankie cried. "Will she do that?"

He shrugged as he swung up into the saddle and laughed. "Let's hope not." He looked good up there, so self-assured, so at home. He spurred his horse forward. "Also, Buttercup's got a crush on Romeo here, so she'll probably just follow him and behave. But you never know with a female." He trotted out of the barn, then reined in to wait for her.

She started to give Buttercup a nudge, but

the mare was already moving after Romeo and Hank.

They rode up into the mountains through towering pines. The last of the summer air was warm on her back. She settled into the saddle, feeling more comfortable than she'd expected to be. Part of that was knowing that she was in good hands with both Buttercup and Hank.

Frankie stole a glance at him, seeing him really relax for the first time since she'd met him. He had his head tilted back, his gaze on the tops of the mountains as if soaking them into his memory for safekeeping. Was he sorry he'd left? It didn't really matter, she realized. He couldn't come back here—not with Naomi's ghost running rampant in his heart and mind. Until he knew what had happened to her, Frankie doubted he would ever find peace.

In that moment, she resolved to find out the truth no matter what it was. She wanted to free this man from his obvious torment. But even as she thought it, she wondered if he would ever really be free of Naomi and his feelings for the dead woman.

"Wait until you see this," Hank said and rode on a little ahead to where the pines opened into a large meadow. She could see aspens, their leaves already starting to turn gold and rust and red even though summer wasn't technically over. This part of Montana didn't pay much attention to the calendar.

As she rode out into the meadow, she was hit with the smells of drying leaves and grasses. It made her feel a little melancholy. Seasons ended like everything else, but she hated to feel time passing. It wouldn't be long before they would be returning to Idaho and their lives there. That thought brought back the darkness that had been plaguing her for the past few months. She was going to have to deal with her past. She only wished she knew how.

Hank had ridden ahead across the meadow. She saw that he'd reined in his horse and was waiting for her at the edge. Buttercup broke into a trot across the meadow and then a gallop. Frankie surprised herself by feeling as if she wasn't going to fall off.

She reined in next to Hank. He was grinning at her and she realized she had a broad smile on her face. "I like Buttercup."

"I thought you might. She's a sweetheart. Except for when she tries to brush you off under a pine tree." His grin broadened.

"You really are an awful tease," she said as he came over to help her off her horse.

"You think so?" he said as he grabbed her by her waist and lifted her down to stand within inches of him. Their gazes met.

Frankie felt desire shoot like a rocket through her. She'd thought she'd put the fire out, but it had only been smoldering just below the surface. She wanted the kiss as much as her next breath.

He drew her closer. "What is it about you that is driving me crazy?" he asked in a hoarse whisper.

She shook her head, never breaking her gaze with his. "I could ask you the same thing."

He chuckled. "I want to kiss you."

She cocked her head at him. "So what's stopping you?"

"I've already had my heart broken once. I'm not sure I'm up to having it stomped on just yet," he said, but he didn't let her go. Nor did he break eye contact.

"You think I'm a heartbreaker?" she said, surprised how breathy she sounded. It was as if the high altitude of the mountaintop had stolen all her oxygen.

He grinned. "I know you are and yet…" He pulled her to him so quickly that she gasped before his mouth dropped to hers.

The kiss was a stunner, all heat. His tongue

teased hers as he deepened it, holding her so tightly against him that she felt as if their bodies had fused in the heat.

He let her go just as quickly and stepped away, shaking his head. "We should get back, but first you should see the view. My mother is bound to ask you at dinner what you thought of it."

She was still looking at the handsome cowboy as she swayed under the onslaught of emotions she didn't believe she'd ever felt before. "The view?" she said on a ragged breath.

Hank laughed and took her hand. "It's this way." He led her to the edge of the mountaintop, still holding her hand in his large warm one. "What do you think?"

She thought that, for a while, they'd both forgotten Naomi. "I've never enjoyed a horseback ride more in my life," she said, her gaze on the amazing view of mountains that seemed to go on forever.

He gently squeezed her hand. "It is pretty amazing, isn't it?"

Chapter Twelve

Dinner was a blur of people and laughter and talk as more relatives and friends gathered around the large dining room table, including Dana's best friend, Hilde, and her family. Fortunately, most of it was going on around Frankie, and all she had to do was smile and laugh at the appropriate times. She avoided looking at Hank, but in the middle of the meal, she felt his thigh brush against hers. She felt his gaze on her. When he placed his hand on her thigh, she wasn't able to control the shiver of desire that rocketed through her. She moved her leg and tried to still her galloping pulse. Getting her body to unrespond to his touch wasn't as easy.

Once the meal was over, she and Hank walked back up to their cabin. For a long way, neither said a word. It was still plenty light out.

"Are you all right?" Hank asked over the evening sounds around them. She could hear

the hum of the river as it flowed past, the chatter of a squirrel in the distance and the cry of a hawk as it caught a thermal and soared above them.

"Fine. You?"

He stopped walking. "Damn it, Frankie. You can't pretend that the kiss didn't happen. That things haven't changed."

She stopped walking as well and turned to face him. Was he serious? They were pretending to be in a relationship and had almost consummated it. Worse, it was all she could think about. And maybe even worse than that, she wanted it desperately. "It hasn't changed anything."

He made a disbelieving face. She wanted to touch the rough stubble on his jaw, remembering the feel of it earlier when he'd kissed her. Not to mention the memory of their naked bodies molded together for those few moments was so sharp that it cut her to the core. "Don't get me wrong. I wanted you more than my next breath. I still do. But—"

"But?" he demanded.

"But you're my employer and this is a job. For a moment we let ourselves forget that."

"So that's the way we're going to play it?" he asked, sounding upset and as disappointed as she felt.

"Let's not forget why we're here. You're still in love with the memory of Naomi after three years of mourning her death. Let's find out who killed her—if she really was murdered—and then…" She didn't know what came after.

"Do you doubt Naomi was murdered after what happened when we left the Corral?" he demanded.

She thought there could be another explanation, though not one she felt she could share with him until she knew for sure. She still wanted to believe that no one knew where she was, especially the man who'd left her dozens of threatening messages on her phone.

Choosing her words carefully, she said, "Based on that and what I've learned about Naomi, I think there is a very good chance that she was murdered."

He stared at her for a moment. "That's right. You haven't told me what you learned about her today." He started walking again as if bracing himself for the worst. "So let's hear it."

HANK LISTENED, GETTING angrier by the moment. They'd reached the cabin by the time she'd finished. "This woman, Tamara Baker, is lying. Naomi hated the taste of booze."

"Tamara insinuated that Naomi was into

something more than booze. Not men. But something more dangerous."

"Like what? Money laundering? Drugs? Prostitution?" He swore. "Stop looking at me like that. Go ahead, roll your eyes. You think I didn't know my own girlfriend?"

"Why would Tamara lie?"

"I have no idea. But she's wrong and so is Roy at the grocery store. Naomi wouldn't steal. He's thinking of the wrong girl. Naomi sure as heck didn't get fired. She was one of his best workers. She showed me the bonus she got for..." His voice trailed off. "I can't remember what it was for, but I saw the money."

Frankie said nothing, which only made him even angrier. He shoved open the door to the cabin, let her go in first and stormed in behind her. "What if it's all a lie to cover up something else?" He knew he was reaching. He couldn't imagine why these people would make up stories about Naomi.

She shrugged. "I only told you what I'd learned. Maybe she had another life when she wasn't with you."

He shook his head and began pacing, angry and frustrated. "You didn't know her. She was afraid of everything. She was...innocent."

"All right, maybe that's how she got involved in something she didn't know how to get out of."

He stopped pacing. "Like what?"

"She had a boyfriend before you, right?"

"Butch Clark. Randall 'Butch' Clark. But she hadn't seen him in years."

"I want to talk to him. Alone," she added before he could say he was going with her.

"Why? I just told you that she hadn't seen him in years."

She said nothing for a moment, making him swear again. "Just let me follow this lead. I'll go in the morning. Any idea where I can find him?"

"His father owns the hardware store. He'd probably know." He felt sick in the pit of his stomach as he recalled something. "He was at Naomi's funeral. I recognized him."

"So you knew him?"

He shook his head. "Naomi pointed him out once when we first started dating. He didn't seem like her type. I asked her about him, but she didn't want to talk about him, saying he was her past."

Frankie nodded knowingly and he caught a familiar glint in her eye.

"I don't even want to know what you're thinking right now," he said with a groan.

She shrugged. "Naomi had a past. That's all."

He cocked his head at her, waiting.

"That she didn't want to talk about," she added. "Happy?"

"You are so sure she had some deep dark secret. I might remind you that you have a past you don't want to talk about."

"True, but you and I aren't dating."

"We're supposed to be," he said, stepping toward her. "I don't see that as being so unbelievable given what almost happened earlier. How about I fire you, end this employer-employee relationship, and we quit pretending this isn't real?"

FRANKIE LOOKED INTO Hank's blue eyes and felt a shiver of desire ripple through her. It would have been so easy to take this to the next level—and quickly, given the sparks that arced between them. Common sense warned her not to let this happen. But the wild side of her had wanted him almost from the first time he'd walked into her office. The chemistry had been there as if undercover, sizzling just below the surface.

Any woman in her right mind would have wanted this handsome, strong, sexy cowboy. She doubted Hank even knew just how appealing he was. Naomi had held his sensuality at arm's length, using herself as a weapon to get him to the altar. Frankie could see that the wild side of Hank wanted out as badly as she wanted to unleash it.

He stopped directly in front of her, so close she could smell the musky outdoor male scent of him. She felt her pulse leap, her heart pounding as she waited for him to take her in his arms.

Instead, he touched her cheek with the rough tips of his fingers, making her moan as she closed her eyes and leaned into the heavenly feel of his flesh against hers.

At a tap on the door, Hank groaned. "If that's my father—"

"Hello?" Dana called. "Are you guys decent?"

Hank swore softly under his breath and then, locking his gaze with Frankie's, grinned. "Come on in, Mom," he said as he grabbed Frankie, pulled her to him and kissed her hard on the mouth. Breaking off the kiss only after the door had opened, he said, "We are now, Mom."

Chapter Thirteen

It was late by the time Dana left. She'd seemed in a talkative mood, and it was clear that she wanted to spend more time with her son. Frankie excused herself to go to bed. She hadn't been able to sleep, though. Her body ached with a need that surprised her. She hadn't felt this kind of desire in a very long time and definitely not this strong.

Trying to concentrate on something, anything else, she considered what she'd learned about Naomi Hill. Sweet, quiet, timid, scared of everything, a nondrinker who was honest as the day was long with only one desire in life—to get married and settle down.

Frankie frowned. Was her reason for giving Hank an ultimatum that night only because of that desire? Or was she running from something?

The thought wouldn't go away. Hours later, she heard Dana leave. She lay on her back, staring up at the ceiling, hardly breathing, wondering if Hank would come to her bed.

He didn't. She heard the creak of the bed in the other bedroom as he threw himself onto it. She smiled to herself hearing how restless he was. Like her, he was having trouble sleeping.

Frankie didn't remember dozing off until she awakened to daylight and the sound of rain pinging off the panes in her window. By the time she'd showered and dressed, determined to do what she had been hired to do, the rain had stopped and the sun had come out. Droplets hung from the pines, shimmering in the sunlight.

When she came out of the bedroom, she found that Hank was also up and dressed.

"I'm going to go talk to Tamara and then maybe go by the grocery store and talk to Roy," he said, not sounding happy about either prospect.

She nodded. He'd shaved and she missed the stubble from last night, but he was still drop-dead handsome. "I'd call you when I get back from seeing Butch Clark, but my phone…"

"Mine too. Why don't we meet back here and have lunch together and share whatever information we come up with? Be careful. I'm sure you haven't forgotten yesterday."

Not hardly. "See you before lunch." She could feel his gaze on her and knew their conversation wasn't over yet.

"About last night—"

"Did you have a nice visit with your mother?"

He grinned, acknowledging that he'd caught her attempt to steer the subject away from the two of them. "I did, but I wasn't referring to yet another interruption just when things were getting interesting. I was going to say, I didn't come to your bed last night not because I didn't want to. Just in case you were wondering. You say you want to keep this strictly professional, but should you change your mind... all you have to do is give me a sign."

She tried to swallow the lump in her throat. He was throwing this into her court. If she wanted him, she'd have to make the next move. Her skin tingled at the thought. "That's good to know," she said and headed for the door.

"No breakfast?" he said behind her. There was humor in his tone, as if he knew she needed to get away from him right now or she might cross that line.

"I'll get something down the road," she said over her shoulder without looking at him because he was right. The thought of stepping into his arms, kissing those lips, letting him take her places she could only imagine, was just too powerful. She turned up the hood on her jacket against the rain and ignored the cold as she kept walking.

HANK SWORE AS he watched Frankie leave. He would have loved to have spent this day in bed—with her. He almost wished he had gone to her bed last night.

As much as he wanted Frankie, he hadn't forgotten why they'd come back to the ranch, back to Big Sky, back to where Naomi had died. He would always love Naomi, he told himself. But for the first time in years, he felt ready to move on. Maybe he could once they'd found out the truth.

He saw his cell phone sitting in the bowl where he'd put it this morning and went to look for Frankie's. He found it beside the sink. It was still wet. He tried to open it. Nothing. Well, at least now she couldn't get those calls that she'd been ignoring.

Who was so insistent? Someone she didn't want to talk to. He'd seen her reaction each time she'd recognized the caller. She'd tensed up as if…as if afraid of the person on the other end of the line? Definitely a man, he thought, and wondered if anyone had ever tried to kill her before yesterday.

He could almost hear her say it went with the job.

But he'd felt her trembling in the water next to him after their escape from his pickup. She'd been as scared as he had been, so he doubted nearly dying went with the job. Although he had a bad feeling that someone *had* tried to kill her. Maybe the person who kept calling.

"Well, now he can't find you, just in case he's been tracking your phone," he said to the empty room.

Hank couldn't put it off any longer. He needed to get to the truth about Naomi. Confronting Tamara and Roy were at least places to start. He wasn't looking forward to it. He doubted they would change their stories, which would mean that he hadn't known Naomi.

He sighed, wishing he was curled up in bed with Frankie, but since that wasn't an option, he grabbed his jacket and headed out into the cool, damp summer morning.

RANDALL "BUTCH" CLARK was easy to find—in the back of his father's hardware store, signing in the most recent order. As the delivery driver pulled away, Butch turned and stopped as if surprised to see that he had company. He was short, average-looking with curly sandy-blond hair and light brown eyes.

"Frankie," she said, holding out her hand as she closed the distance between them.

Butch hesitated. "If this is about a job, my dad does the hiring. I'm just—" He waved a hand as if he wasn't sure exactly what his title was.

"I'm not looking for a job. I'm here about Naomi."

"Naomi?" he repeated, both startled and suddenly nervous as he fiddled with the clip-board in his hands. "Is there something new with her that I don't know about?"

Frankie decided to cut to the chase. "I'm a private investigator looking into her death." If he asked for her credentials, she was screwed. Fortunately, he didn't.

His eyes widened in surprise. Or alarm? She couldn't be sure. "Why? It's been three years. I thought her death was ruled a sui-cide?" His voice broke.

She closed the distance between them, watching the man's eyes, seeing how badly he wanted to run. "You and I know it wasn't suicide, don't we, Butch?"

"I don't have any idea what you're talking about."

Frankie went on instinct based on Butch's

reaction thus far. He was scared and he was hiding something. "You and Naomi were close." She saw him swallow as if he feared where she was headed. "So if anyone knew what was going on with her, it was you."

Butch didn't deny it. "Why are you asking about this now?"

"The marshal has reopened the case."

He took a step back, put down the clipboard on one of the boxes stacked along the delivery ramp and wiped his palms on the thighs of his dirty work pants. "Look, I don't want to get involved."

"You're already involved, Butch. But I might be able to help you. No one needs to know about your...part in all this if—" he started to object but she rushed on "—you tell me what you know. The marshal didn't question you the first time, right?" She saw the answer. Hud hadn't known about the old boyfriend. "So there is no reason for your name to come up now, right?"

His eyes widened in alarm. "I didn't do *any-thing.*"

"But Naomi did."

He looked down at his scuffed sneakers.

"Could we sit down?" she asked and didn't wait for an answer. There were three chairs around a folding card table that appeared to be used as a break room. Probably for the smokers since there was a full ashtray in the middle of the table along with several empty soda cans.

"Just tell me what you know and let me help you," she said. "I'm your best bet."

He pulled out a chair, turned it around and straddled it, leaning his chin on his arms as he looked at her with moist brown eyes. "I don't even know who you are or who you work for."

"Probably better that you don't if you want me to keep your name out of it, but—" She reached for her shoulder bag.

He quickly waved it off. "You're right. I don't want to know. But if you work for them, I had nothing to do with this. I told her not to keep the money. It was like she'd never seen a movie and known that they always come after the money."

Frankie did her best not to let her surprise show as she quickly asked, "Where did she find it?"

"She told me on the highway." His tone said he didn't believe her.

"Did she tell you how much money was in it?"

He looked away. "I told her not to count it. Not to touch it. To put it back where she found it and keep her mouth shut. But she saw there was a small fortune in the bag. She'd never seen that much money."

"What did she plan to do with it?"

Butch let out a bark of a laugh. "Buy a big house, marry that rancher she was dating, move down here in the valley, raise kids, go to soccer practice. She had it all worked out except…" He shook his head.

"Except?"

He looked at her as if she hadn't been listening. "The rancher didn't want to marry her, she thought someone was following her and she ended up dead."

Frankie caught on two things he'd said. Butch knew that the night of Naomi's death, Hank said he wasn't ready to get married. Someone was following her that night. "Did she tell the rancher about the money?"

"No way. She said he was too straitlaced. He'd want to turn it in to his father. He'd be too scared to keep it."

But timid little Naomi apparently wasn't. "You said someone was following her?" He glanced down, obviously just realizing what he'd said. "The night she died. That's when you talked to her."

He looked up but she shook her head in warning for him not to lie. "She called the bar where

I was having a drink with friends and told me that she thought she was being followed."

"What did you tell her to do?"

He rubbed a hand over his face. "I didn't know what to tell her. She sounded hysterical. I said give it back. Stop your car, give it to them. She said she couldn't, that she'd put some of the money down on a house and couldn't get it back."

"So then what did you tell her to do?"

"I thought that maybe if she explained the situation…"

Frankie groaned inside. If the money Naomi had found was what she thought it was, negotiating was out of the question. "So she pulled over and tried to bargain?"

He shrugged, his voice breaking when he spoke. "I don't know. The line went dead. I tried to call her back but there was no answer."

"Did she know who she'd taken the money from?" Frankie asked.

"If she did, she never said anything to me. I swear it." He rose from the chair. "Please, I thought this was over. I thought your people… Whoever you're working for. I thought they got most of their money back. At least, what was left." He frowned. "I thought it was over," he repeated.

Frankie got up from her chair. "As far as I'm concerned, it is over."

Relief made him slump and have to steady himself on the back of the chair he'd abandoned. He let out a ragged breath and straightened. "So we're good?"

She nodded as a loud male voice called from inside the store.

"That's my father. I have to—" He was gone, running through the swinging doors and disappearing from sight.

Frankie went out the back way and walked around to the pickup Dana Savage had lent her. Climbing behind the wheel, she wished she had a cell phone so she could call Hank. Up the block she spotted the time on one of the banks. It was about forty minutes back to Big Sky. She'd tell Hank when she saw him. But at least now she knew the truth.

Naomi Hill had been murdered—just as he'd suspected. It didn't put them any closer, though, to knowing who'd killed her, but at least now they knew why.

HANK DROVE INTO Meadow Village after he left the ranch. Frankie had told him that Tamara worked at the Silver Spur Bar. But when he parked and went inside, he was told that it was her day off. He asked for her address and wrangled for a moment with the bartender before the man gave it over. Hank dropped a twenty-dollar bill on the bar as he left.

He knew the old cabins the bartender had told him about. But as he neared the row of four cabins, he spotted marshal office vehicles parked out front. Crime scene tape flapped in the wind.

Swearing, he pulled in and, getting out, started past the deputy stationed outside.

"Hold up," the deputy said. "No one goes inside. Marshal's orders."

"Tell him I need to see him," Hank said. He held up his hands. "Tell him his son is out here, Hank. Hank Savage. I'll stand right here until you get back and won't let anyone else get past. I promise."

The deputy disappeared inside and almost at once returned with Hud.

"What's going on?" Hank asked in a hushed voice as the two of them stepped over to the ranch pickup he'd driven into town.

"What are you doing here?"

"I came by to see Tamara Baker. Frankie had spoken to her about Naomi. I wanted to talk to her." Immediately he realized his mistake as he saw his father's eyes narrow. "Tamara said some things about Naomi that didn't seem right."

"Like what?"

He didn't really want to discuss this out here, let alone voice them at all, especially to his father. Also, the marshal hadn't answered his question. He pointed out both.

"Tamara's dead."

"Dead? Not—" He didn't have to say "murdered." He saw the answer in his father's expression.

"When I get through here, I think we'd better talk." With that, his father turned and went back inside as the coroner's van pulled up.

Chapter Fourteen

Back at the ranch, Frankie went straight to
the cabin to wait for Hank. She felt anxious.
What she'd learned was more than disturbing.
Naomi had apparently found the answer to her
prayers—or so she thought. Where had she
picked up the bag of money? It seemed doubt-
ful that it had been tossed out beside the road.

At the sound of the door opening, she spun
around and saw Hank's face. "What's happened?" she asked, feeling her pulse jump and
her stomach drop.

"I went over to talk to Tamara Baker. She
wasn't at the bar. I got directions to her cabin.
My father was there along with a crime team
and the coroner." He met her gaze. "She'd
been murdered."

The news floored her. Stumbling back, she
sat down hard on the sofa. The ramifications
rocketed through her. She'd talked to Tamara
and now she was dead. Swallowing down the

lump in her throat, she said, "There's more. I'm pretty sure I know why Naomi was murdered."

Hank moved to a chair and sat down as if suddenly too weak to stand. "You talked to Butch."

"He said she found a bag of money."

"What?" he asked in disbelief.

"Drug money, I would imagine. Enough money that she put some of it down on a house in Bozeman for when the two of you got married."

He dropped his head into his hands. "This can't be true," he mumbled through his fingers.

"She called Butch that night at the bar where he was meeting his friends—"

"So this bastard knew about this the whole time?" Hank demanded as his head came up, his blue eyes flaring.

"She told him she was being followed. She was afraid it was them, whoever the money belonged to. She debated stopping and giving back what she had left with a promise to pay back the rest."

He groaned. "She was going to make a deal with a bunch of drug dealers?"

"Her phone went dead. He tried to call her back but there was no answer."

Hank shook his head. "She told him all of this? So he knew she was in trouble and he didn't do anything?"

Frankie knew that the tough part for Hank was that Naomi hadn't trusted him with her secret. It wasn't just that she'd been living a lie, the bonus at work, not telling him about getting fired, the drinking with Tamara, the close connection with her old boyfriend when she felt she was in trouble, and River Dean, the backup if things didn't work out with Hank.

It was a lot for the cowboy to take. She wondered how Naomi had planned to explain all this money she'd come into, including the house she was in the process of buying. Maybe an inheritance? Maybe Hank would have bought the explanation, except that he hadn't wanted to get married and move to Bozeman.

Naomi had been so naive that she'd thought the drug dealers wouldn't find out who'd taken their money? Especially if it had been a lot. A small fortune to Naomi might not have been that much to some people in the wealthy part of Big Sky. But the drug dealers would have wanted it back.

"I suspect, given what you just told me," Frankie said, "that Naomi also confided in Tamara."

Hank pushed to his feet, a hand raking

through his hair as he walked to the window, his back to her. "I didn't know her at all." He sounded shocked. "I loved her so much and I had no idea who she really was."

"You loved the idea of her. You fell in love with what she wanted you to see. Eventually, you would have seen behind the facade. Hopefully, before it was too late to walk away unscathed."

HANK HEARD SOMETHING in her voice. Regret. He turned to study Frankie. "Is that what happened with this man who keeps calling you?" He didn't expect an answer. He thought of Naomi. "I'm not sure it was love—at least on her part. With love comes trust. She didn't trust me enough to tell me about the money."

"Your father is the marshal."

He let out a snort. "She really thought I'd go to my father with this?"

"Wouldn't you have?"

Hank laughed and shook his head. "I would have made her turn the money over to my father." He nodded. "It would have been the only smart thing to do and she would have hated me for it."

Frankie gave him a that's-why-she-didn't-tell-you shrug.

"Well, he has to know about all of this now.

He probably has people he suspects are dealing drugs in the area. What are the chances that they killed Naomi and now Tamara?" His gaze came up to meet hers and his quickly softened. "You can't blame yourself."

"I talked to her and now she's dead. Who should I blame?"

"The man you said was sitting down the bar. He was the only witness when the two of you were talking, right?"

She nodded. "But she could have told someone after that."

He shook his head as all the ramifications began to pile up. "I knew she'd been murdered. I damn well knew it. But I would never have guessed..." He sighed. "When I saw my father at Tamara's cabin, I told him that you'd talked to Tamara about Naomi. I'm sorry. I slipped up."

"Don't you think it's time we tell your parents the truth? It's pretty obvious that we're investigating Naomi's death."

"Come on. Let's go." He headed for the door.

"Just like that?"

He shook his head. "My father could be here any moment. Let's go get some lunch. I don't want to be interrogated on an empty stomach."

They left the ranch with him driving the

ranch pickup he'd borrowed that morning. "I know this out-of-the-way place." He turned onto the highway and headed south toward Yellowstone Park.

Lost in thought, he said little on the drive. He could see that Frankie was battling her own ghosts. He wondered again about the man in her life who kept calling. All his instincts told him that the man was dangerous.

As he neared the spot they would have lunch, he dragged himself out of his negative thoughts, determined to enjoy lunch with Frankie and put everything behind them for a while.

"My father and grandfather used to tell stories about driving down here in the dead of winter to get a piece of banana cream pie," he said as they turned into a place called the Cinnamon Lodge. "It used to be called Almart. Alma and Art owned it and she would save pieces of banana cream pie for them."

"That's a wonderful story," Frankie said, as if seeing that he wanted to talk about anything but Naomi. "Something smells good," she said as they got out and approached the log structure.

Hank figured she wasn't any more hungry than he was. But he'd needed to get out of the cabin, away from all of it, just for a little while. It wasn't until after they'd had lunch and were in the pickup again that he told her what he'd been thinking from the moment he saw the crime scene tape around Tamara's cabin.

"It's time for you to go back to Idaho. You can take one of the pickups and—"

"I'm not leaving," she said as he started the pickup's engine, backed out and pulled onto the highway.

"You don't understand. You're fired. I have no more use for your services."

FRANKIE LAUGHED AND dug her heels in. "You think you can get rid of me that easily?"

"I'll pay you the bonus I promised you as well as your per diem and—"

"Stop! You think I don't know what you're doing?"

He glanced over at her, worry knitting his brows. "It's too dangerous. I should have realized that after what happened yesterday with that truck. But now that we know what we're dealing with—"

"Exactly. What *we're* dealing with. I want to see this through. With you." Her last words broke with emotion.

Hank sighed and reached for her, pulling her over against him on the bench seat of the older-model pickup. She cuddled against him, finding herself close to tears. She couldn't quit this now. She couldn't quit Hank. "Frankie—"

She touched a finger to his lip. "I'm not leaving."

"Yesterday was a warning," he said. "I see that now. If we don't quit looking into Naomi's death—"

"Her *murder*," she said, drawing back enough to look at him. "Are you telling me that you can walk away now that you know the truth?" She could see that he hadn't thought about what he would do.

"We have no idea who they are. Unless my father can track down that truck and find the driver…"

"So you think that makes us safe? You think they won't be worried about what we know, what we found out?"

"I don't want to think about it right now." He pulled her close again, resting his head against the top of hers for a moment as he drove.

She could hear the steady, strong thump of his heart as she rested her head against his chest. This man made her feel things she'd never felt before. Together there was a strength to them that made her feel safe and strong… and brazen.

"Then let's go back to the cabin and not think at all," she said, taking that unabashed step into the unknown as if she was invincible in his arms.

HANK MEET HER gaze and grinned as he slowed for the turnoff to the ranch. "Are you making a move on me, Miss Brewster?"

She sat up and started to answer when she looked out the windshield at the road ahead and suddenly froze. Following her gaze, he could see a large dark sedan parked on the edge of the road into the ranch. He looked over at Frankie as she moved out from under his arm to her side of the pickup. All the color had drained from her face.

"Frankie?" he asked as he made the turn into the ranch and drove slowly by the car. He could see a man sitting behind the wheel. Frankie, he noticed, hadn't looked. Because, he realized, she knew who it was.

"Frankie?" Her gaze was still locked straight ahead, her body coiled like a rattler about to strike.

"Stop," she said and reached for her door handle.

He kept going. "No way am I letting you face whatever that is back there alone."

She shot him a desperate look that scared

him. "Damn it, Hank, this has nothing to do with you. Stop the pickup and let me out. *Now!*"

Frankie was right. He'd opened up his life to her, but hers had been off-limits to him from the get-go. Nothing had changed.

He gritted his teeth as he brought the pickup to a stop. Her door opened at once and she jumped out, slamming the door behind her as she started to walk back to where the car and driver waited.

Watching in the side mirror, he cursed under his breath as he remembered her frightened expression every time her cell phone had rung with a call from whoever the man had been. Hank would put his money on that same man now sitting in that car, waiting for her.

All his instincts told him that whoever this man was, he was trouble. Frankie could pretend he wasn't, but Hank knew better. Except that she'd made it abundantly clear she wanted to handle this herself.

With a curse, he shifted into gear and headed the pickup down the road toward the ranch. She didn't need his help. Didn't want it. The PI thought she could handle this herself. She probably could.

After only a few yards up the road, he slammed on the brakes. Like hell he was going to let her handle this on her own, whether she liked it or not.

Throwing the pickup in Reverse, he sped back up the road, coming to a dust-boiling stop in front of the car.

Frankie had almost reached the vehicle. He saw that the driver had leaned over to throw the passenger-side door open for her to get in. The jackass wasn't even going to get out.

He could hear the man yelling at her to get in. Grabbing the tire iron from under the seat, Hank jumped out.

"She's not getting into that car with you," he said as he walked toward the driver's-side window. He could feel Frankie's angry gaze on him and heard her yell something at him, but it didn't stop him. "You have a problem with Frankie? I want to hear about it," he said, lifting the tire iron.

Chapter Fifteen

The man behind the wheel of the car threw open his door and climbed out. He was as tall as Hank and just as broad across the shoulders. The man had bully written all over him from his belligerent attitude to the bulging muscles of his arms from hours spent at the gym. Hank heard Frankie cry, "J.J., don't!"

"Who the hell are you and what are you doing with my fiancée?" the man she'd called J.J. demanded.

Hank shot a look at Frankie across the hood of the man's car.

"She didn't mention that she's engaged to me?" J.J. said with obvious delight. "I see she's not wearing her ring either. But you haven't answered me. Who the hell are—" His words were drowned out by the sudden *whop* of a police siren as the marshal pulled in on the other side of Hank's pickup.

J.J. swore. "You bitch," he yelled, turning to glare at her. Frankie had stopped on the other side of his car. She looked small and vulnerable, but even from where he stood, Hank could see that she would still fight like a wild woman if it came to that. "You called the law on me?"

The man swung his big head in Hank's direction. "Or did you call the cops, you son of a…" He started to take a step toward Hank, who slapped the iron into his palm, almost daring him to attack.

J.J.'s gaze swung past him. Out of the corner of his eye, he saw his father standing in front of his patrol SUV. J.J. saw the marshal uniform as well, swore and hurriedly leaped back into his car. The engine revved and Hank had to step back as J.J. took off, tires throwing gravel before he hit the highway and sped away.

"What was that about?" Hud asked after he reached in to turn off the siren before walking over to his son.

Hank looked at Frankie, who was hugging herself and shaking her head. "It was nothing," he said. "Just some tourist passing through who wanted to give us a hard time."

His father grunted, clearly not believing a

word of it. "I need to talk to the two of you. Your cabin. Now."

Hank nodded, his gaze still on Frankie. "We'll be right there."

J.J. DROVE AWAY, fuming. *She called the cops on me?* Had she lost her mind? And that cowboy... Hank Savage had no idea what he'd stepped into, but he was about to find out.

"The cowboy's name is Hank Savage. His father's the marshal of the resort town of Big Sky, Montana," his friend at the station told him after he'd managed to get the license plate number off one of the business surveillance cameras near Frankie's office. The camera had picked up not just the man's truck but a pretty good image of the cowboy himself going into Frankie's office and coming out again—with her. She'd gone down the block, gotten into her SUV and then followed the pickup.

"You recognize the cowboy?" his friend had asked.

"No. It must be a job." But she'd left her rig in her garage.

"Well, if it is a job, she went with him, from what you told me her neighbor said."

That was the part that floored him. Why would she take off with a man she didn't know? Unless she did know him. He thought of how the man had defended her. Hell, had she been seeing this cowboy behind his back?

He drove down the highway, checking his rearview mirror. The marshal hadn't come after him. That was something, anyway. But how dare his cowboy son threaten him with a tire iron. That cowboy was lucky his father came along when he did. He swore, wanting a piece of that man—and Frankie. He'd teach them both not to screw around with him.

He pulled into the movie theater parking lot and called his friend back in Lost Creek. After quickly filling him in, he said, "I'm going to kill her."

"Maybe you should come on back and let this cool down until—"

"No way. I don't know what's going on, but she's my fiancée."

Silence. Then, "J.J., she broke off the engagement. You can't force her to marry you."

"The hell I can't. Look, she's mad at me. I screwed up, got a little rough with her, but once we sit down and hash this out, she'll put the ring back on. I just can't have some cowboy get in the middle of this."

"Where'd she meet this guy?"

"That's just it. I have no idea. Why would she just leave with him unless she knew him before? The neighbor said she packed a small bag and left. If she'd been seeing this cowboy behind my back, I would have heard, wouldn't I?"

"It's probably just what you originally thought. A job."

He shook his head. "She was sitting all snuggled up next to him in the pickup. It's not a job. The bitch is—"

"Come back and let yourself cool down. If you don't, you might do something you're going to regret. You already have a couple strikes against you at work. You get in trouble down there—"

"Not yet. Don't worry. I'll be fine." He disconnected. Fine once he got his hands on Frankie. He sat for a moment until he came up with a plan. He'd stake out the ranch. The next time she left it, he'd follow her. But first he had to get rid of this car. He needed a nondescript rental, something she or the cowboy wouldn't suspect.

"I DIDN'T WANT you involved," Frankie said with rancor the moment they were in his pickup, headed back to the ranch. The marshal had waited and now followed them into the ranch property.

"You made that clear. None of my business, right?" He looked over at her, his eyes hard as ice chips. "It isn't like you and I mean anything to each other. Still just employer and employee. Why mention a fiancé?"

"I told you, I broke it off."

He continued as if he hadn't heard her. "It isn't like we were just heading up to our cabin to… What was it we were going to do, Frankie?"

She sighed and looked away. "J.J. and I were engaged. I called it off two months ago. He didn't take it well."

"So I gathered. Now he's still harassing you. Why haven't you gone to the authorities?"

"It's complicated. I don't have the best relationship with the local cops in Lost Creek."

"Because you're a private investigator?"

"Because J.J. is one of them. He's a cop."

"A cop?" Hank shook his head. He was driving so slowly, he knew it was probably making his father crazy. It was his own fault for insisting he follow them into the ranch. As if he thought they might make a run for it?

"How long did you date him?"

"Six months. He seemed like a nice guy. The engagement was too quick but he asked me at this awards banquet in front of all his friends and fellow officers. I… I foolishly said yes even though I wasn't ready. Even though I had reservations."

"He doesn't seem like the kind of guy who takes no for an answer." When she said nothing, he added, "So he put a ring on your finger and then he wasn't a nice guy anymore. Nor does he seem like a guy who gives up easily." Hank met her gaze.

She dragged hers away. "It's his male pride. All his buddies down at the force have been giving him a hard time about the broken engagement. It isn't as if his being unable to accept it has anything to do with love, trust me. He just refuses to let this go. I gave him back his ring and he broke into my house and left it on my dining room table. But this isn't your problem, okay? I'll handle it."

He shook his head. "He comes back, *I'll* handle it," he said. "I can see how terrified you are of him and for good reason. I asked you if he was dangerous. I know now that he is. That man's hurt you and next time he just might kill you. I'm not going to let that happen as long as you're—" their gazes met "—in my employ," he finished.

After parking next to his father's patrol SUV, he sat for a moment as if trying to calm down. He'd been afraid for her. She understood he'd been worried that she would have stupidly gotten into that car.

Through the windshield, she could see the marshal was standing next to his patrol SUV, arms crossed, a scowl on his face as he waited.

Beside her in the pickup cab, she could feel Hank's anger. "Right now I don't even know what to say to you. Would you have been foolish enough to climb into that car with that man?" He glanced over at her. "You make me want to shake some sense into you until your teeth rattle. Worse, you stubbornly thought you could handle a man like J.J. and didn't need or want my help."

She wanted to tell him that she'd been on her own for a long time. She wasn't used to asking for help, but he didn't give her a chance.

"I thought you trusted me," he said, his voice breaking with emotion as he parked in front of the house and climbed out.

FOR A MOMENT, Frankie leaned back against the seat, fighting tears. Hank had shot her a parting look before getting out and slamming the door behind him. It was filled with disappointment that wrenched at her heart. He'd thought she was smart. Smart wasn't getting involved with J.J. Whitaker. Worse was thinking she could handle this situation on her own. Hank was right. J.J. was dangerous. If he got her alone again, he would do more than hurt her, as angry as he was.

Wiping her eyes, she opened her door and followed the two men up the mountain to the cabin. She ached with a need to be in Hank's arms. J.J. had found her at the worst possible time. Had he been delayed a few hours, she would have been curled up in bed with Hank. Instead, Hank was furious at her, and with good reason.

She should have told him the truth way before this. J.J. was a loose cannon. What would have happened if the marshal hadn't come along when he did? She just hadn't thought the crazed cop would find her. Why hadn't she realized he would use any and every resource he had at his disposal to get to her? Especially if her nosy neighbor had told him that she'd left with some cowboy.

J.J. would have been jealous even if her relationship with Hank were strictly business because he thought every man wanted what he had. With Hank acting the way he did…well, J.J. would be convinced she and Hank were lovers. They would have been, she thought as a sob bubbled up in her chest and made her ache.

Not that it would have solved anything. In fact, it would have complicated an already difficult situation. But now she was drowning in regret.

Chapter Sixteen

The marshal and Hank were both waiting for her when she topped the hill at the cabin. Hank held the door open for her and his father. She walked past him, feeling his anger and his fear. She'd told him to let her handle it and yet he'd come back to save her. She loved him and wanted to smack him for it.

"Anyone else want a beer besides me?" Hank asked as he went straight to the kitchen. His father declined as he took a seat in the living area. Frankie could have used something stronger, but she declined a beer as well. She felt as if she needed to keep her wits about her as she sat down on the couch.

"You want to tell me what that was about on the highway?" Hud said quietly to Frankie since he'd already heard Hank's version.

"An old boyfriend who won't take no for an

answer," she said. "He's a cop in Lost Creek, where I live. He tracked me here."

The marshal nodded. "He going to be a problem?"

She swallowed. "I hope not."

Hank came back into the room carrying a bottle of beer, half of it already gone. "If he comes back here—"

"You call me," Hud interrupted. "You call me and let me handle it. I mean it."

Hank said nothing, his face a mask of stubborn determination mixed with anger. She couldn't tell how much of it was anger at her for not telling him or wanting to handle it herself or being frustrated by the J.J. situation as well as the two of them and where they'd been headed earlier.

The marshal cleared his voice. "We found the truck that ran you off the road. It's an old one that's been parked up at an abandoned cabin. Lab techs are checking for prints, but they're not hopeful. Anyone who knew about the truck could have used it. I'm surprised the thing still runs. Anyway, the paint matched as well as the damage to the right side."

"So it was someone local," Hank said. He looked at Frankie and saw her relief that it hadn't had anything to do with her and J.J. The woman had so many secrets. He thought of Naomi and cursed under his breath. Except Naomi had been needy. Frankie was determined to handle everything herself. He shook his head at her and turned back to his father.

"That makes sense given what we've learned about Naomi's death," he said and looked to Frankie again to see if she wanted to be the one to tell him. She gave him a slight nod to continue.

She was on the couch, her legs curled under her with one of Hank's grandmother's quilts wrapped around her. He could tell that her run-in with her former fiancé had rattled her more than she'd wanted him to see.

He was still angry and had a bad feeling that J.J. might come to the ranch next time looking for her. He'd obviously tracked her as far as the main entrance. How crazy was the cop? Wasn't it enough that they had drug dealers wanting to kill them?

"Naomi found a bag of money," Hank began and told his father what Frankie had found out about Naomi's final phone call to an old boyfriend saying she was being followed and asking him what she should do. Give what money she had left back? "And then apparently her phone went dead or she turned it off."

Hud swore under his breath. "Drug money?"

"That's the assumption."

"Did this old boyfriend, whose name I'm going to need, did he say where she'd found it?" He looked to Frankie. She shook her head. "And you knew nothing about this?" he said, turning back to Hank.

"Nothing." He chewed at his cheek for a moment, trying to hold back his hurt and anger, realizing that he was more angry at Naomi than Frankie, though both had kept things from him. He was aware of the distinction between the two. Naomi was his girlfriend, the woman he'd planned to marry. Frankie... He looked over at her. She was a hell of a lot more than his employee—that much he knew. "Apparently Naomi didn't trust me. Must be something about me that women don't trust."

Frankie groaned and shook her head. "Let's leave you and me out of this."

He saw his father following the conversation between them with interest for a moment before getting back to Naomi and the drug money.

"If she had told you, I hope you would have been smart enough to come to me. Wouldn't you?"

Hank nodded. "I certainly wouldn't have let her keep the money, which I'm sure is why she didn't tell me."

"So the two of you have been digging around in Naomi's death," Hud said after a moment. Hank glanced over at Frankie and considered telling his father about his arrangement with the PI. But he had a feeling his father already knew. Anyway, their arrangement was beside the point.

"Tamara must have at least suspected who the drug dealers were," Hank said.

"And contacted them to let them know that we were asking questions," the marshal said.

"Would explain how we ended up in the river."

"I'm pretty sure she was involved." They both looked over at Frankie, surprised that she'd spoken.

"You talked to Tamara," Hud said. "Did you get the feeling she knew more than she was telling you?"

"She hinted that Naomi was wilder than anyone knew, that she had secrets and lived a double life. But from what Hank had told me about her," Frankie continued, "I had the feeling Tamara was talking about herself."

"Well, whatever she knew, she is no longer talking," the marshal said. "And the two of you…" He took a breath and let it out. "I wish you'd been honest with me about what you were doing."

"You didn't believe that Naomi had been murdered," Hank pointed out, feeling his hackles rise a little.

"I know, and I'm sorry about that. You were right. I was wrong. But now you have to let me handle this. I need you both to promise that you're done investigating."

"I promise," Hank said, looking at Frankie.

"Fine," she said. "If that's what you want," she said to him, rather than the marshal.

"Do you have some suspects?" Hank asked.

"I hear things," his father said. "The problem is getting evidence to convict them. Are there drugs being distributed in Big Sky? Maybe even more than in other places in Montana just because of the amount of money here." He rose to leave. "I'm expecting you both to keep your promise. Otherwise, I'm going to lock you up. I'm tempted to anyway, just to keep you both safe. As much as I hate to say this, it might be a good idea for the two of you to go back home to Idaho. At least for a while."

Hank looked at Frankie. "We'll leave in the morning."

"After breakfast. Your mother will be upset enough, but at least have one more meal with her before you take off," Hud said and met Hank's gaze. "You might want to tell your mother the truth. I don't want her planning a wedding just yet."

Hank walked his father out. "Dad, that car earlier? It was Frankie's former fiancé. She broke up with him two months ago but he's continued to stalk her. He's a cop from Lost Creek."

"I'll keep an eye out for him."

"Thanks." He felt his father's gaze on him and seemed about to say something but must have changed his mind.

"See you at breakfast," Hud said, turned and left.

FRANKIE FELT AS if her heart would break. She felt ashamed. She should have known better with J.J. She'd ignored all the red flags. It made her more ashamed when she remembered how she'd given Hank grief for ignoring the obvious signs with Naomi. She prided herself on reading people, on seeing behind their masks, on using those skills to do her job.

But when it came to her own personal life? She'd failed miserably. It didn't matter that J.J. had hidden his real self from her. She still should have seen behind the facade. Now she couldn't get away from him. He must have tracked her phone. How else could he have found her? At least he hadn't tried to kill them in that old truck that forced them into the river. She could be thankful for that.

Throwing off the quilt, she headed for the shower, feeling dirty and sick to her stomach. She'd never wanted Hank to know about J.J., let alone have the two meet. After turning on the shower, she stepped under the warm spray and reached for the body gel to scrub away her shame and embarrassment.

Tomorrow she and Hank would go back to Idaho. She hated leaving anything unfinished. She'd at least found out why Naomi Hill had died. But she had no idea who might be behind the murder. As she tilted her face up to the water, she remembered the man sitting at the end of the bar the day she went to talk to Tamara. He'd been acting like he wasn't paying them any attention, but he'd probably been listening to their conversation. Also, Tamara had gone down the bar and the two had been whispering. What if he was—

The shower door opened, making her spin around in surprise, all thoughts suddenly gone as she looked into Hank's baby-blue eyes. "Mind if I join you?"

She stepped back and watched as he climbed in still dressed in everything but his boots. "You don't want to take off your clothes?"

"Not yet," he said as he closed the shower

door behind them and turned to take her in. "Damn, woman, you are so beautiful."

"I'm so sorry that you had to find out about J.J.," she said, close to tears. "He's the big mistake of my life and I'm so ashamed for getting involved with such a loser."

He touched his finger to her lips and shook his head. "We all make mistakes. Look at me and Naomi. But you don't have to worry. I'm not going to let J.J. hurt you ever again. I promise."

"I don't want you—"

"Involved? Once I take off my clothes and get naked with you? We'll be in this together, you understand?"

She swallowed the lump in her throat, but could only nod.

He slowly began to unsnap his Western shirt.

"I think you'd better let me help you with that," she said, grabbing each side of the shirt and pulling. As the shirt fabric parted, revealing his muscled, tanned chest, she ached to touch him. As he drew her to him, she pushed her palms against the warmth of his flesh and leaned back for his kiss.

"Last chance," Hank said as he ended the kiss and reached for the buttons of his jeans.

"There won't be any going back once these babies come off."

She laughed and pushed his hands away to unbutton his jeans and let them drop to the floor of the shower along with his underwear and his socks. She looked at his amazing body—and his obvious desire—and returned her gaze to his handsome face. "No going back," she said as she stepped into his arms again and molded her warm, wet body to his.

HANK KISSED HER passionately as he backed her up against the tiled wall of the shower, before his mouth dropped to her round, full breasts. Her nipples were dark and hard, the spray dripping off the tips temptingly. He bent his head to lick off a droplet before taking the erect nipple into his mouth and sucking it.

Frankie leaned her head back, arching her body against his mouth, a groan of pleasure escaping her lips. He took the other nipple in his mouth as his hand dropped down her belly and between her legs. He felt her go weak as his fingers found the spot that made her tremble. She clung to him as he made slow circles until she cried out and fell into his arms again.

He reached around to turn off the water and opened the shower door. After grabbing several large white bath towels from the hooks, he tied one around his waist and wrapped Frankie in the other. Sweeping her into his arms, he carried her toward his bedroom. His heart pounded. He meant what he'd told her. They were now in this together. No more secrets.

She looped her arms around his neck and leaned her face into the hollow of his shoulder as he kicked open the door to the bedroom, stalked in and, still holding her, kissed her, teasing her lips open with his tongue. The tip of her tongue met his and he moaned as he laid her on the bed.

She grabbed him and pulled him down with her. "I want you, Hank Savage," she said, the words like a blaze she'd just lit in his veins. "Oh, how I want you."

MUCH LATER THEY lay in each other's arms, Frankie feeling as if she was floating on a cloud. She couldn't remember ever feeling this happy, this content. But there was another emotion floating on the surface with her. She had trouble recognizing it for a moment because it was so new to her. Joy.

It made her feel as if everything was going to be all right. She usually wasn't so optimistic. She was too rational for that. But in Hank's arms, she believed in all the fairy tales. She even believed in true love, although she knew it was too early to be thinking this way. Look at the mistake she'd made with J.J. Six months hadn't been long enough to date him before getting engaged.

She looked over at Hank. And here she was curled up in bed with a man she'd only known for days.

"Are you all right?" he asked as she sat up to sit on the edge of the bed.

The reality of it had hit her hard. "I was just thinking this might be too fast."

He caressed her bare back. "I can understand why you're scared, but is that what your heart tells you?"

Gripping the sheet to her chest, she turned to look at him. She knew only too well what her heart was telling her. She just wasn't sure she could trust it right now.

Finding safer ground, she said, "I remembered something when I was in the shower— before you joined me. The man sitting at the bar. He was more than a regular. He and Tamara…they had a connection. I'm sure of it and it wasn't romantic. He had to overhear our conversation, which could mean…that if he was involved in the drug distribution and Tamara knew about it or was involved, he could have ordered the driver of that truck to either scare us or kill us."

"You're purposely avoiding the question."

Frankie gave him an impatient look. "Sandy blond, about your height, a little chunkier." That made him raise a brow. "You know what I mean."

Hank stopped her. "I know who you're talking about. I know exactly who you're talking about. I went to school with him. Darrel Sanders. He has a snow removal business in the winter. I have no idea what he does in the summer." He reached for his phone and realized the late hour. "I'd better wait and tell Dad at breakfast."

He drew her back onto the bed, turning her to spoon against her. "We can take all the time you want," he whispered into her ear, sending a shiver through her. "I'll wait."

She pressed her body against his in answer and felt his desire stir again. Chuckling, she turned in his arms to kiss him. He deepened the kiss and rolled her over until she was on top of him.

Frankie looked into his blue eyes and felt so much emotion that it hurt. Too fast or not, she was falling hard for this cowboy.

Chapter Seventeen

Dana noticed right away that there was something different about her son and Frankie. She shot a look at Hud. He shrugged, but as he took his seat at the breakfast table, she saw him hide a knowing grin. She knew that grin.

"So, how are you two this morning?" she asked, looking first at her son, then Frankie.

"Great," they both said in unison and laughed.

She noticed that they were sitting closer together, and if she wasn't wrong, her son's hand was on Frankie's thigh. Whatever problems they'd been having, she was relieved to see that they'd moved on from them. At least for the time being. She feared that the ghost of Naomi was still hanging around.

"I made a special breakfast," she said. "Waffles, eggs, ham and bacon, orange juice and fresh fruit."

"Mom, you shouldn't have gone to all this

trouble," Hank said, "but we appreciate it. I'm starved." He picked up the plate of waffles, pulled three onto his plate and passed the plate to Frankie.

"I can't remember the last time I had waffles," Frankie said and helped herself.

"Try the huckleberry syrup," he suggested. "It's my grandmother's recipe. Or there is chokecherry syrup, also my grandmother Mary's recipe." Dana had named her daughter after her.

She loved seeing her son and Frankie in such a good mood. She watched with a light heart as they helped themselves to everything she'd prepared. They both did have healthy appetites. She smiled over at Hud, remembering how he'd appreciated hers, back when she was that young.

She looked at the two lovebirds and wondered, though, if she'd really ever been that young. Nothing could spoil this moment, she thought, right before the phone rang.

Hud excused himself to answer it since it was probably marshal business.

Hank got up too, to follow his father into the other room.

Dana pushed the butter over to Frankie. "You look beautiful this morning. I love that shirt." It wasn't one of those baggy ones like she wore most of the time.

"Thank you." Frankie looked down at the shirt as if just realizing that she'd put it on that morning. When she looked up, her eyes clouded over.

"I'm sorry—was it something I said?"

"No, it's just that I love being here and—"

Hank came back into the room, followed by his father. Dana saw their expressions and said, "What's happened?"

Hud put a hand on his wife's shoulder. "It's just work, but Hank and Frankie are going back to Idaho today. They're leaving right after breakfast."

Dana shook her head as she felt her eyes burn with tears. "So soon?" she asked her son. "It feels like you just got here."

"It's for the best right now," Hank said. "We both have jobs to get back to, but don't worry. I'll be home again before you know it."

Her gaze went to Frankie as she recalled how close the young woman had been to tears just moments ago. Because she knew they were leaving? Or because she wouldn't be coming back?

"She'll be coming back too," Hank said quickly as if reading her expression. Her son sat back down at the table to finish his breakfast and gave Frankie a look that was so filled with love, Dana felt choked up.

"I certainly hope you'll both be back," she said, fighting tears.

"I have to go," her husband said as he leaned down to give her a kiss on the cheek. She reached back to grab his hand and squeeze it. She wished he would retire. There were days he left the house when she wasn't sure he would make it home alive again. It was a thought that filled her with fear. She couldn't wait for the days when the two of them would be here together on the ranch with their grandchildren and the phone wouldn't ring with marshal business.

"You told your dad about the man I saw at the bar?" Frankie asked as they left the ranch house.

"Darrel Sanders." He nodded as they walked up to the cabin to get their things.

She could tell that leaving here was hard on Hank. Probably because it was so hard on his mother. "Your mom is so sweet."

"Yeah, she is. Frankie, I know all this is new between us, but I have to be honest with you. Being here, it makes me wish I'd never left. I miss it."

She nodded. "I can see that."

"Not because of Naomi. Maybe in spite of her. I miss my family. I miss ranch work."

"There's no reason you shouldn't come back. This is your family legacy." Frankie could feel his gaze on her.

"You have to know that if, down the road, once you've had enough time to accept that we belong together..."

"What are you saying?" she asked, stopping on the trail to face him.

"That if my coming back here was a deal breaker with us, I would stay in Idaho and I would be fine at my job."

She shook her head. "I would never keep you from what you love or your family. But we still need to slow down. This is way too fast."

"Not for me, but I can see it is for you. Plus we still have to deal with your ex-fiancé. I get it. Like I told you, I'll wait." He leaned toward her, took her face in his big hands and kissed her. "Umm, you taste like huckleberries."

She saw the look in his eye and laughed. Why not? It wasn't as if they were in a hurry to get back to Idaho.

As HANK DROVE out of the ranch, he couldn't help looking back. Frankie noticed and reached over to put her hand on his thigh.

"You'll be back."

He nodded. "*We'll* be back."

She smiled and looked out her window. He realized she was looking in her side mirror.

His gaze went quickly to his rearview mirror. No sign of J.J. "Let's hope he gave up and went back to Idaho."

"I doubt it. But since that's where we're headed…"

"What are we going to do about him when we get back?"

"I've hesitated to get a restraining order because, one, I know it won't do any good, and, two, it will only infuriate him and make things worse."

He stole a look at her as he drove. He still couldn't believe this. He was crazy about her. She was all he'd thought about. But the J.J. situation scared him. They weren't out of the woods yet. Until J.J. was no longer a problem, he and Frankie couldn't move forward. "What other option is there?"

"Short of shooting him?" She brushed her hair back. This morning she'd tied back her long mane. Tendrils had escaped and hung in a frame around her face. She couldn't have looked more beautiful.

"I understand why he doesn't want to lose

you. I feel the same way. But his methods are so desperate, so…"

"Insane?" She nodded. "Also his reasons. He wants me back to save face. If he loved me he wouldn't—" Her voice broke.

"I'm guessing he's been violent with you," he said as he drove away from Big Sky headed north.

She nodded without looking at him. "Please, I don't want to talk about him. It's a beautiful day and I don't want to spoil it."

It was. A crisp blue cloudless sky hung over the tall pines and rocky cliffs of the canyon. Beside them, the river flowed, a sun-kissed clear green. He felt her gaze on him.

"Are you all right with leaving? I mean, we came here to—"

"Because I was convinced Naomi was murdered. We have good reason now to believe it's true. It's up to my father now to find out the truth."

She nodded. "It feels unfinished."

He glanced over at her. "Once we knew what Naomi had gotten involved with, it was too dangerous to stay because I know you. You wouldn't stop looking. I couldn't let you do that. It was getting too dangerous. Not to mention my father would have locked us up if we continued to investigate it."

FRANKIE STARED AT him in surprise. "But you wouldn't have stayed and kept looking if I wasn't with you."

"I just told you. My father would have probably thrown me in jail is what would have happened."

"Hank—"

"There is no way I'm putting you in that kind of danger."

"That isn't your choice. This is what I do for a living."

"I've been meaning to ask you how you came to be a private eye."

She could see that he was changing the subject, but she answered anyway. "I had an uncle who was a private investigator. I started out working for him in his office. He took me on a few cases. I was pretty good at it. When he moved to Arizona and closed his office, I opened mine." She shrugged. "I kind of fell into it. Would I do it over? I don't know." She looked at him. "That day we went on the horseback ride up into the mountains?" He nodded. "I felt the kind of freedom I've always felt with my job. It was…exhilarating. If I could find a job that let me ride a horse every day…"

"As a rancher's wife, you could ride every day."

She'd been joking, wanting to change the

subject. But now she stared at him and saw that he was completely serious. They hadn't even said that they loved each other and he was suggesting she become his wife.

But as she looked at him, she knew it in her heart. She did love him. She'd fallen for him, for his lifestyle, for his family. She'd fallen for the whole ball of wax and now he was offering it to her?

Frankie looked away. As she did, she saw the man stagger out into the highway. "Hank, look out!"

HANK HIT THE BRAKES. The pickup fishtailed wildly, but he got it stopped before he hit the man who'd dropped to his hands and knees in the middle of the highway.

He threw open his door, jumped out and rushed to the man gasping for breath, whose face was smeared with blood.

"Help me," the man said. "My car went off the road back in the mountains."

Hank reached down to help him up. Traffic had been light. What few drivers passed slowed down to look, but didn't stop.

"Here, let me help you to my pickup," he said as he half lifted the man to his feet. As they approached the passenger side, Frankie moved over to give him room to climb in with Hank's help.

After closing the door, Hank hurried around to slide behind the wheel. "I can take you to the hospital in Bozeman."

"That won't be necessary," the man said, no longer wheezing.

Hank shot a look at the man and felt his eyes widen as he saw the gun now pressed to Frankie's temple.

"Drive up the road," the man ordered. "I don't want to kill her, but I will."

Chapter Eighteen

J.J. had parked down the road from the ranch turnoff. He'd been able to see anyone coming or going. Stakeouts were something he was good at because he required so little sleep. He was usually wired. Catching bad guys was his drug of choice.

Catching Frankie and straightening her up was enough motivation to keep him awake for days. His dedication paid off in spades this morning when he saw the pickup coming out of the ranch with both the cowboy and Frankie.

The pickup turned north and J.J. followed in the SUV he'd rented. It cost him a pretty penny to rent, but he would spare no expense to get Frankie back. As he drove, he admitted to himself that he'd made mistakes when it came to her. He'd put off the actual wedding, stringing her along for a while because while he liked the idea of having her all to himself, he wasn't ready to tie himself down.

He'd been happy knowing that no other man could have her as long as she was wearing his ring. So when she'd wanted to break up, he'd been caught flat-footed. He'd thought it was because he hadn't mentioned setting a date for the wedding. But in that case, he would have expected her to start talking about making wedding plans or leaving bride magazines around or dropping hints and crying and giving him ultimatums.

Instead, she'd said she didn't want to marry him, that the engagement had been a mistake and that she wanted out. She'd handed him his ring. Hadn't even flung it at him in anger.

That was when he'd gotten scared that she was serious. No recriminations, no tears, just a simple "I don't want to marry you. I'm sorry."

It had hit him harder than he'd expected. He'd been relieved, and yet the thought of her just tossing him back like a fish that didn't quite meet her standards really pissed him off. He'd thought, *Like hell you're going to walk away from me.*

He'd gotten physical. But what guy wouldn't have under those conditions? That was when she stopped answering his calls, refused to see him, basically cut him off entirely. At first, he thought it was just a ploy to get him to the altar. Of course she wanted to marry him. He was a good-looking guy with a cool job. Didn't all women go for a man in uniform?

Since then he'd been trying to get her back every way he could think of. But it became clear quickly that she was serious. She wanted nothing more to do with him. That was when he got mad.

Now, as he followed the pickup north out of town, he considered what to do next. He had no idea where they were headed. But wherever they were going, they didn't seem to be in a hurry.

It was early enough that traffic was light, so he stayed back, figuring he couldn't miss them if they stopped anywhere in the canyon. Once out of it, he'd have to stay closer. After his all-night stakeout, he wasn't about to lose them now.

They were almost out of the canyon when he saw the pickup's brake lights come on. He quickly pulled over to see what was going on. There was no place for them to turn off, so what the—

That was when he saw the cowboy jump out and rush up the road. A few moments later, the cowboy returned and helped a man into the passenger side of the truck. The man appeared to be injured.

As the pickup pulled back onto the highway, so did J.J. This put a new wrinkle in things, he thought. When not far out of the canyon, the cowboy turned off before the town of Gallatin Gateway. Maybe they were taking the man to his house on what appeared to be the old road along the river. Still, it seemed strange.

J.J. followed at a distance, telling himself this might work out perfectly for him. When they dropped the man off, maybe that was when he'd make his move.

"What is this about?" Hank asked, afraid he knew only too well.

"You'll find out soon enough," the man said. "Right up here around the next corner, take the road to the left toward the mountains."

Hank couldn't believe he'd fallen for this. But in Montana, you stopped to help people on the road. He hadn't given it a second thought, though he regretted that kindness now.

He shot a look at Frankie. She appeared calm, not in the least bit worried, while his heart was racing. The man had a gun to her head! He couldn't imagine anything worse, and then realized he could. At least Frankie wasn't standing on a ledge over the river, looking down at the rocks, knowing she was about to die.

He saw the turn ahead and slowed to take it, glancing into his rearview mirror. There was a vehicle way back on the road. No way to signal that they needed help.

They were on their own. He knew they would have to play it by ear. He would do whatever it took to keep Frankie safe—even if it meant taking a bullet himself.

He turned onto the road. As it wound back into the mountains, he told himself that it made no sense for the drug dealers to kidnap them, let alone kill them. They'd gotten away with murder for three years. If he and Frankie had uncovered evidence against them, they would have been behind bars by now.

So why take them? That was the part that made no sense. Running them off the road had been a warning to back off, but this…this terrified him. Maybe they were cleaning up loose ends, like with Tamara, since she obviously had known more than she'd told Frankie.

THE FIRST THING the marshal did when he left the ranch after breakfast was drive over to Darrel Sanders's house. He'd hoped to catch him before he got up. He remembered the boy

Darrel had been as a classmate of Hank's. A nice-looking kid with a definite chip on his shoulder.

Darrel had moved into his mother's house after she died. It was a small house in a subdivision of other small houses away from Meadow Village.

But when he pulled up, he saw that Darrel's vehicle, an old panel van, was gone. He tried his number, let it ring until voice mail picked up before hanging up.

It made him nervous that Darrel wasn't around. The man worked in the winter but, as far as Hud could tell, did nothing in the summer to earn a living. The supposition was that he made so much with his snow removal business that he had summers off.

Hud sat for a moment, letting his patrol SUV idle in front of the house before he shut off the engine, got out and crossed the yard. He'd always gone by the book. But there was no way he could get a warrant based on what he had, which was simply suspicion.

At the house, he knocked and then tried the door. Locked. Going around the small house, he tried to look in the windows, but the curtains were pulled.

At the back, he stepped up onto the small porch. A row of firewood was stacked head high all along the back side of the house and down the fence, cutting off any view of most of the neighbors.

Hud tried the back door and, finding it locked, he put his shoulder into it. He wasn't as young as when he used to do this. The door held and his shoulder hurt like hell, but he tried again.

The lock gave and he opened the door and quickly stepped in, telling himself that he smelled smoke and thought he'd better check to make sure nothing was on fire inside. A lie, but one he would stand behind. The inside of the house wasn't as messy as he'd expected it to be. He'd wondered if Darrel had gone on the lam after Tamara's death, but if he'd packed up and taken off, there was no sign of it.

A pizza box sat in the middle of the table. He opened it and saw that several pieces were still inside. There were dishes in the sink and beer in the refrigerator. He had the feeling that Darrel hadn't gone far.

He thought about waiting for him, but after looking around and finding nothing of interest, he left by the way he'd come in, feeling guilty and at the same time vindicated.

He'd insisted before Hank left that he get a new cell phone before he left town. He tried his number now.

FRANKIE STARTED AS Hank's cell phone rang. She hadn't replaced her own, saying she'd take care of it once she got home. She wanted a new number, one that J.J. probably wouldn't have any trouble getting, though. That thought had come out of nowhere. A foolish thought to be worrying about J.J. when a stranger had a gun to her head.

Hank's cell rang again.

"Don't touch it," the man ordered, pressing the barrel of the gun harder against her temple and making her wince.

"It's probably my father, and if I don't answer it, he'll be worried and put a BOLO out on us."

The man swore. "Give me your phone." Hank dug it out and handed it over. The man stared down at it for a moment and said, "Answer it. Tell him you're fine but can't talk because of the traffic and will call him later. Say anything more and the last thing your father will hear is this woman's brains being splattered all over you. Got it?"

"Got it." He took the phone back and did just as the man had told him before being ordered to hand the phone back.

Frankie watched the man pocket the phone. She hadn't been able to hear the other side of the conversation. But it appeared the marshal had accepted that Hank couldn't talk right now.

She took even breaths, letting herself be lulled by the rocking of the pickup as Hank drove deeper into the foothills. She knew better than to try to take the gun away from the man in these close quarters. She would wait and bide her time. She hoped Hank was on the same page. He appeared to be since he hadn't tried to get a message to his father.

They came over a rise and she saw a small cabin set back against rocks and pines. Several rigs were parked in front of it, including a panel van that she'd seen before. It took her a moment to remember where. In front of the Silver Spur Bar in Big Sky. Darrel Sanders's rig. So this was just as they suspected, about the drug money and Naomi's death.

"Park over there and then we're going to get out very carefully," the man said. "This gun has a hair trigger. If you try anything—"

"I get the picture," Hank said impatiently. "But now this. If you shoot her, you'd better shoot me as quickly as possible because if you don't—"

"I get the picture," the man interrupted, and she saw him smile out of the corner of her eye.

Even knowing what this was about, she couldn't understand why they were being brought here. She didn't think it was to kill them, but she knew she could be wrong about that. The thought made her breath catch and her mouth go dry. She and Hank had just found each other. She had hardly let herself believe in this relationship. She didn't want it to be over so soon—and so tragically.

She'd said she needed time, but even after her bad experience with J.J., she knew in her heart that Hank was nothing like the cop. He was the kind of man who made a woman feel loved and protected. The kind of man who loved horses and wanted to make babies and raise a family.

Frankie felt tears burn her eyes as she let herself admit that she wanted that as well. Wanted to come back here to the ranch and raise their kids here. She wanted Hank.

The man opened his door and grabbed her with his free hand to pull her out of the pickup, the gun still pointed at her head. Hank had gotten out on the other side of the pickup and stood waiting, his gaze on the man as if hoping for an opportunity to get the gun away from him.

She willed Hank to look at her, and when he shifted his gaze, she smiled, hoping to reassure him that they were going to get through this. They had to. She'd seen their future and she wasn't ready to give that up. If it meant a fight…well, she was ready.

"WHAT A CHUMP," J.J. said as he looked after Hank and Frankie. He couldn't believe how accommodating the fool was. First he picked up a complete stranger from the middle of the road and then what? Offered to drive him home? And his home ended up being way down a dirt road, back in the foothills?

J.J. had gone on past the turnoff when he'd seen the pickup begin working its way back into the foothills. After turning around, he'd found a place to park, pulled his gun out of the glove box, checked to make sure it was fully loaded, then stuck it in the waistband of his jeans as he got out of the rental car.

It might be a hike back in to wherever the cowboy had taken the man, but J.J. thought the area couldn't be more perfect for what he had in mind. Even if they dropped the man off and were headed back this way before he reached the man's house on foot, he could work with it.

Feeling as if Lady Luck had smiled on him, he couldn't imagine a more perfect place to end this. Once he explained things to the cowboy, he hoped that was the end of any problem from him.

Frankie was his. Period. End of discussion.

True, right now she was giving him some trouble, but he would try humbling himself, sweet-talking her, spoiling her, and if that didn't work then he'd have to get physical. It wasn't something he wanted to do, but she had to understand how things were going to be. She couldn't embarrass him in front of his friends and his coworkers. She had to behave. No one respected a man who couldn't keep his woman under control.

Once they established the rules, hell, maybe he'd suggest they pick a wedding date. Marrying her might be the only way to keep her in line. If that was what he had to do, then he'd bite the bullet and get it over with. It wasn't like he had someone else he wanted to marry. There were some he wanted to get into bed, but he could do that easily enough after he was married to Frankie. She had to understand that he had his needs. Real men did.

J.J. was feeling good as he headed up the road. He'd gone a quarter mile when he realized that he couldn't hear the sound of a vehicle engine anymore. He came over a rise and saw why.

In the distance was a small cabin with four rigs parked in front of it, including the cowboy's pickup. What he didn't see was any sign of Frankie or the cowboy, though. Maybe the man they'd rescued had invited them in for something. A drink to pay them back for saving him?

Fine with J.J. He was in no hurry. He kept to the trees along the edge of the foothills until he was close enough to the cabin that he would see them when they came out.

Maybe he'd just hitch a ride with them when they left, he thought, feeling the weight of the gun pressing against his stomach. He pulled it out and sat down on a rock to wait, thinking about the future he and Frankie would have. Everything was going to be fine now. Like his boss had warned him, he just needed to get his life under control or he could be in trouble at work.

The memory made him grit his teeth. This was all Frankie's fault. But he would get the bitch in line—one way or the other.

THE MAN LED them into the cabin at gunpoint. Hank stepped through the door, Frankie and the man behind him, the gun still to Frankie's head. The cabin appeared larger on the inside than it had from outside. At a glance he took it all in as his mind raced for a way out of this that didn't get them both killed.

He saw a small kitchen against one wall, a bed and a half-dozen mismatched chairs around a table. Darrel was sitting in one of the chairs. A large man he didn't recognize was standing against the wall, looking tough. Hank didn't miss the holstered gun visible under the man's jacket.

He went on the defensive, determined not to let him see how worried he actually was. "What the hell, Darrel?"

His former classmate smiled. "Sit down, Hank. There's no reason to get all worked up. Les," he said to the man they'd picked up in the middle of the highway, "why don't you and Frankie sit over there." He pointed to the bed. "That way we can all see each other."

Hank hadn't moved. Darrel kicked out one of the chairs across the table from him. "Take a load off and let's talk."

"I can't imagine what we might have to talk about."

"Hank, we've known each other for too long to lie to each other. So let's cut the bull. You know perfectly well why you're here. Sit."

Hank took the chair, turning it around to straddle the seat and rest his arms on the back. He'd be able to move faster this way—if he got the chance.

Darrel smiled, seeing what Hank was up to, but said, "Your father was by my house this morning looking for me and snooping around,

I heard. I suspect it's your doing. Yours and your—" his gaze shifted to Frankie "—your lady friend's." He eyed Frankie with interest for a moment before turning back to Hank. "Picked yourself up a private eye, did you? Why would you do that?"

He considered several answers before he said, "I never believed that Naomi killed herself."

Darrel nodded with a grimace. "No, you never did."

"So I hired Ms. Brewster to help prove I was right."

"And did you?" He could feel the man's intense gaze on him.

"No. Suspecting is one thing. Proving is another. It's why Frankie… Ms. Brewster and I were leaving town." He didn't want Darrel thinking there was anything more between him and Frankie than employer and employee. He knew the man well enough to know he would use it against them.

Darrel raised a brow in obvious surprise. "Leaving? Giving up that easy? Just doesn't sound like you, Hank. Remember how you were when it came to competitive sports? You couldn't stand to let me win. So why give up now?" His former classmate seemed to consider it for a moment before his gaze swung to Frankie. "Things get a little too complicated for you?"

He saw no reason to lie. "They did. So we decided to put all of this behind us and go back to our lives in Idaho."

Darrel shifted his weight to lean across the table toward him. "I'm happy for you. Personally, I thought you were never going to get over Naomi, but apparently you've now found a woman who's made you forget her. Under normal circumstances, I'd wish you well. But here is the problem. I still want my money that your former girlfriend stole. I thought it was lost forever, but then you came back to the canyon and I figured, 'Hank's come back to pick up the money. He was in on it the whole time.' I actually admire you for waiting three years. I kept track of you and knew you hadn't spent it. For a while, I thought maybe Naomi hadn't even told you about it. So where is it? In your pickup? Trent, go take a look."

"Wait a minute," Frankie said, making them all turn to look at her. "Naomi didn't have the money on her that night, the night you killed her?"

Chapter Nineteen

As J.J. had approached the cabin, he considered climbing in the back of the cowboy's
pickup. From the hill where he sat, he could
see that there appeared to be some old tarps
in the back. He could hide, and when the time
was right, he could pop up. *Surprise!*

The idea had its appeal. He just wasn't sure
he could reach the pickup before they came
out, and given the number of vehicles parked
outside the cabin, he couldn't be sure how
many people were inside.

The rock where he sat was far enough away
that he could see the cowboy and Frankie
when they came out, but they probably
wouldn't notice him. It wouldn't take much
for him to trot down to the road and stop them
once they were out of sight of the cabin.

They seemed to have been in there for a
while now, he thought, frowning. Maybe the
man was more injured than he'd thought.

What if they'd sent for an ambulance? Worse, the cops?

But as time passed with no sign of either, he was beginning to wonder what could be going on inside that cabin. Maybe he should get a little closer. The rock he was sitting on wasn't that comfortable anyway, he thought as he began to work his way down the hillside through the pines.

The front door of the cabin opened. He jumped back behind a pine, thinking it was about time they came out. But the man who emerged wasn't the cowboy. He was a big, tough-looking dude. Sunlight caught on the gun in the man's holster.

What the hell?

J.J. watched as the man went straight to the cowboy's pickup. It didn't take long to understand what was going on. The man was searching the truck. He obviously didn't find what he was looking for—even after going through their bags behind the seat. When he slammed the pickup door, he glanced at the tarps in the back and quickly climbed in to search there as well.

"Glad I wasn't under one of those tarps," J.J. said to himself as he watched the man finish his search and go back inside the cabin.

Something was definitely wrong and Frankie

was in there. He considered what to do. No way was he busting in there, gun blazing. The way he saw it, all he could do was wait. Maybe if he heard screams from Frankie, he might have to change his mind.

Since the man had searched the pickup, it made sense that he wouldn't be looking in the back again. He continued down the hill, keeping his gun ready and his eyes focused on the cabin door.

Staying low, he made his way through the vehicles to the cowboy's pickup and leaped into the back, covering himself with the tarps to wait.

TRENT RETURNED MINUTES later from searching the truck. "Not there."

Frankie watched Darrel's jaw muscle bunch as the tension in the room became thick as smoke. But beside her, Les had released her arm and now merely sat with the gun pressed into the side of her head.

"I thought we were going to be straight with each other," Darrel said, clearly trying to contain his anger.

Frankie could see that Hank was getting angrier by the moment. "That was you the day at the river," Hank said. "That was you I saw running through the trees."

"I followed you thinking you were going for the money. Instead, you were doing what you always did, sitting and staring at that cliff. Three years, I've waited. When you came back after all this time, I thought it was finally to get the money."

Hank shook his head. "You had us forced off the road and into the river. You could have killed us."

"I doubted you would die, but at that point, you hadn't gone for the money and I was losing patience."

"When are you going to get it through your head?" Hank demanded. "We don't have your money. Now let us go."

"I don't think you realize your circumstances," Darrel shot back as he got to his feet and limped over to where Les had his gun to Frankie's head. He grabbed a handful of Frankie's dark hair in his fist as a switchblade suddenly appeared in his other hand. Frankie cried out in pain as he jerked hard on her hair, exposing her throat to the knife.

"I could cut her throat right now, and I will if you don't stop lying to me."

Hank leaped to his feet and took a step toward him. Behind him, Trent moved too quickly. She felt Darrel release her hair and turn.

"Don't!" Darrel yelled at Trent, but his command wasn't quick enough. The man had pulled his gun and now brought the barrel down hard on Hank's head.

Frankie screamed and jumped to her feet, only to be pulled back down by Les.

Darrel swore as Hank toppled to the floor. From where Les held her, she could see that his head was bleeding.

"Help him!" she cried.

Darrel, still swearing, limped over to him and checked for a pulse. "He's not dead." Hank moaned and struggled to sit up. "Get a towel for his head," he ordered. "Now!" Trent disappeared into the bathroom. "Everyone just calm down. I don't like things to get violent but I'm tired of being lied to. I want my money." He said the last through gritted teeth.

"Hank doesn't know where your money is," Frankie said, her voice breaking. She could see that he was dazed and bleeding, but alive. At least for now.

"Tie him up," Darrel ordered when Trent returned with the towel. He tossed the towel to Hank, who put it against the side of his head and flinched.

"Is that necessary?" Frankie demanded. "He's injured. He needs to go to the hospital, not be tied up." She got a warning side look from Darrel.

"You both brought this on yourselves," he said. "Maybe you didn't know about the money, but obviously you do now. So stop lying. Since Hank and Naomi were going to get married and she had put money down on a house, don't tell me he doesn't know where she hid the rest of it."

Trent pulled out duct tape and, after helping Hank into a chair, bound him to it.

"I told you, I don't know," Hank mumbled and seemed to be fighting unconsciousness.

"I know who has your money," she said.

Hank's head came up. He shot her a pleading look. "Frankie—"

She turned her gaze on Darrel, who slowly swiveled around to look at her. "If you're lying, something much worse is going to happen to you. Do you understand?"

"Perfectly. But there's something I need to know first."

"You don't seem to be in a position to be making ultimatums," Darrel said, sounding almost amused.

"You're wrong. I'm the only person in this room who can get you your money." Darrel glanced at Hank. "He doesn't know," she said. "So if you didn't find the money on Naomi that night, then you're right—she hid it somewhere. But what I don't get is why you killed her before she told you where."

He seemed to consider whether to answer or not, and then swore. "One of my associates was handling it and made an error in judgment."

"That's what you call killing her?" Hank said through clenched teeth. She could see he was in pain from the head wound. "An error in judgment?"

"Tamara didn't kill her," Darrel said. "She took her up on the ledge to scare her since she knew Naomi was afraid of heights. All Naomi had to do was tell her where the money was. It wasn't in her vehicle. Nor her apartment, which had already been searched. We suspected it was hidden on the ranch, but we needed the location. Naomi refused to give it to her. Tamara argued with her. Naomi tried to push past her on the ledge to leave, making it clear that she was never going to tell. She took a misstep and fell to her death. Killing her was the last thing we wanted to do."

"Until you got the money," Frankie said. She could see that Hank was struggling to stay conscious, struggling with the news about Naomi.

"You both misjudge me," Darrel said. "Dead bodies complicate things. I prefer not to shed blood unless I have to. Unfortunately, some of my other associates are less reasonable." He rose unsteadily from his chair, and Frankie was reminded of his limp when he'd come into the bar.

Stepping back, he lifted his pant leg to expose a mass of red and purple scar tissue. When he spoke, there was fury in his voice. "You have no idea how much your former girlfriend has cost me, and not just in money and pain. I came close to getting my throat cut— and that would have been the faster and least painful in the long run, I realize now. My associates had much worse plans for me. I've been busting my ass for three years to pay them back. I've been waiting for you to return to town to collect the money after that foolish, stubborn woman took it and refused to tell us where she'd hidden it. Now," he said as he covered his injured leg again and slowly lowered himself into his chair.

He turned his attention to Frankie. "You say you know who has my money?"

She nodded. "One more question first, though," she said, making him groan. She knew she was trying his patience, but she also knew that she had leverage and she planned to use it. She had to use whatever she could to get them out of this. "How was Naomi able to steal the bag of money that she referred to as a small fortune? I would have thought you'd be watching it closer than that. Unless she was one of your associates."

Darrel laughed at that. "Hardly. She and Tamara had become friends. Naomi gave Tamara free groceries and even money out of the till sometimes when she came in and no one else was around." He swung his gaze back to Hank. "Your girlfriend was a shoplifter. Did you know that? She got her kicks by stealing. Tamara failed to mention that until later when my money went missing."

"So you didn't know who took it at first," Frankie said.

"No," Darrel admitted. "I waited to see who started spending."

Frankie thought of the house that Naomi had put a down payment on, hoping Hank would marry her. "How much money are we talking?" she asked.

Darrel shook his head.

"So you knew that Naomi had a larcenous streak and yet you left it lying around?"

Darrel gave her a warning look and then said, "I didn't leave it lying around. I'd brought the money to the bar that afternoon to meet someone. The person was running late and some men came into the bar. I didn't like their looks. I sensed trouble, so I hightailed it into the office. Unfortunately, I didn't have time to put the money into the safe. So I stuck it behind some liquor boxes. Two men jumped me as I walked out of the office. They didn't get far in their plan, but in the confusion of throwing them out of the place with some help from a couple of friends…the money disappeared."

"How did you know Naomi took it?"

He sighed. "It took a little while to figure it out. I had to go through a few possibilities first. In the end, Tamara and I both remembered Naomi being in the bar and disappearing when the trouble started. Tamara thought Naomi might have gone to the restroom before the fight broke out. My office is right across from the women's bathroom. When I heard she'd put money down on a house in Bozeman… Now, no more questions. Who has my money?"

Frankie thought of Randall "Butch" Clark. It hadn't taken much to get the truth out of him and that had worried her at the time. He'd seemed scared enough, but he had wanted her to believe that Naomi had the money on her that night. That she was thinking about stopping and giving the drug dealers what she had left.

But it seemed he'd lied about that. Still,

she didn't want to get him killed. "I'm going to take you at your word that you're not into bloodshed," Frankie said, getting to her feet. Les leaped up as well as he tried to keep the gun on her and get a better grip on her. She didn't think he would shoot and knew she was taking a chance, but she'd bluffed her way this far. "Tell him to get that gun out of my face."

Darrel looked from her to Les. "Sit down, Les. I have a gun under the table. I can kill them both if necessary. You can put your piece away." He turned his gaze on her. "You have a lot of guts. He could have killed you just then before I could stop him."

She had a feeling that Les wasn't that quick-thinking, but kept it to herself. "Let me get this straight. Naomi didn't have the money on her that night, right?"

"I believe we already covered that."

"Tamara was following her that night, right? So what if she had the money and Tamara lied? She killed Naomi and kept the—"

"Tamara didn't have the money," Darrel said, talking over her. "Trust me, some of my more bloodthirsty associates talked to her about this at length before she…expired. She stuck to her story. Tamara took her up on the ledge to force her to tell what she did with it, but Naomi refused. Then the stupid woman slipped and fell."

HANK FELT AS if he was in a nightmare, one of his own devising. If he hadn't come back here, if he hadn't brought Frankie, if he'd just let Naomi go. His head ached and his vision blurred.

Frankie was scaring him, but he didn't know how to stop her—especially injured and bound to a chair.

"But if Naomi was being followed, how could she have dumped the money before she stopped or was pulled over?" Frankie asked.

Darrel shrugged. "You tell me."

"She'd already hidden the money," Frankie said, nodding as if to herself. "She called someone to tell the person where the money was in case something happened to her."

Frankie was right. Naomi had hidden the money and called the person she trusted—her old boyfriend, Butch. It was the only thing that made any sense. Naomi thought the money was safe. She didn't think the drug dealers would really kill her until they had it. If she hadn't slipped—

He felt Darrel's gaze on him. "That's exactly how I saw it. She hid the money and made a call to tell her lover where he could find it. How about it, Hank? Isn't that the way you see it?"

"Naomi didn't call Hank," Frankie said.

But Hank knew who Naomi had called—and so did Frankie. He looked at her and felt his heart drop. He could see what she was thinking, but wasn't sure how to head her off.

"Why wouldn't Naomi tell on that cliff?" Hank demanded, stalling for time, afraid that Frankie was only about to get herself in deeper. "That makes no sense." And yet he knew. He didn't even have to look at Frankie and see that she knew too. He felt his stomach drop.

"She wasn't giving up the money," Frankie said, sounding sad for the woman she'd been investigating and sad for him. "It meant that much to her."

He shook his head, unable to accept that he'd never really known Naomi. He knew that she'd always felt deprived and wanted desperately to have the life she dreamed of having. Still, he didn't want to believe that she would put money before her own life.

"That's crazy. She's standing on the edge of the ledge over the river and she'd rather die than give up the money?" he said.

No one said anything, but he saw that Darrel was staring at Frankie.

Hank felt as if he was on a runaway train with no way to stop it. No way to jump off either.

"I can get you your money," Frankie said to Darrel. "But you're going to have to let me leave."

"Frankie, no," Hank said, feeling dizzy. "You can't trust him." He let out a curse, feeling helpless and scared. "You can't expect him to stick by any deal, Frankie. He used to cheat at every sport I ever played with him."

Darrel shook his head at Hank but he was smiling. "I had to cheat. You were too good for me. But right now, I think I have the upper hand."

"Frankie—"

"Put some tape over his mouth," Darrel ordered, and Trent sprang to it.

Hank tried to put up a fight but it was useless. He felt weak even though he hadn't lost that much blood. He wondered if he had a concussion. Right now his only concern, though, was Frankie. He'd foolishly gotten to his feet, knowing that Trent was behind him. He hadn't expected the man to hit him. Neither had Darrel. Now he found himself duct-taped to a chair and gagged. And Frankie was about to make a deal that could get her killed.

SHE'D KNOWN HANK wasn't going to like this and would have tried to stop her if he could have. "Let me go get your money," she said again to Darrel.

"Do I look stupid? If I let you go, you'll hightail it straight to the authorities, and the next thing I know, there'll be a SWAT team outside my door."

"You have another option?" Frankie asked. "We can't tell you where the money is because we don't know. We didn't even know about it until recently. If you kill us, you'll never get the money and Hank's father will never stop looking for you. Stupid would be making your situation worse. Can't you see we're trying to help you figure this out?"

Darrel shook his head. "You make it sound like if you hand over the money, we all just walk away as if nothing ever happened. I just kidnapped the two of you."

"You are merely detaining us," Frankie said. "Until you get your money. Then you'll let us go. No harm, so to speak," she said, looking pointedly at Trent, "no foul. That's the deal."

"Trent goes with you."

She shook her head. "Not a chance. I go alone. It's the only way I have a chance of getting the person who took your money to admit the truth."

"How do I know you'll come back?"

"I'll come back. You have Hank."

"Good point," Darrel said. "I just wasn't sure you were that invested in him. If you don't come back, he dies. You call in the cops—"

"Save your breath. I'm not going to the authorities, but I need your word that he'll be safe until I get back," she said. "No more tough-guy stuff. The thing is, I don't know how long it will take me."

"You'd better not be playing me."

Frankie met Darrel's gaze. "You want your money. Hank and I want to get on with our lives." Her gaze went to Hank. He gave a small shake of his head and looked pointedly at Trent leaning against the wall again. Frankie knew this was dangerous, but she could see only one way out. Hank was already injured. She could imagine all of this going south quickly if she didn't do something. But what she was suggesting was a gamble, one she had no choice but to take.

"I'll give you until sundown."

Frankie shook her head. "I might need longer. Like I said, this could take a while."

Darrel shook his head. "Sundown or he's dead."

She wanted to argue but she could see she'd pushed the man as much as he was going to take. "Sundown, but promise me that I won't be followed. You need to trust me to handle this."

Darrel wagged his head. "You're asking a lot, sweetheart."

"It's Frankie. And I have a lot to lose," she said and looked at Hank. "There's one more thing that I need," she said to Darrel. "A gun."

Chapter Twenty

All of her bravado gone, Frankie's hands were shaking as she climbed into the pickup. She laid the unloaded gun on the seat next to her. Darrel said he wasn't about to hand her a loaded gun.

"I'm taking one hell of a chance on you as it is," he'd said. "I give you a loaded gun…" He'd smiled as he'd shaken his head. "I'm betting a whole lot on you as it is, lady."

It was mutual, she thought now. She'd just gambled Hank's life on her suspicion of what had happened to the stolen drug money. What if she was wrong? Even if she was right, the money could be gone. Or Butch might refuse to give it to her. For all she knew, he could have gone on the lam after she'd talked to him at his father's hardware store.

Hank was depending on her. She drove toward Bozeman, checking behind her for a tail, trying not to speed for fear of being pulled over. She considered calling the marshal, but couldn't risk it. Not yet, anyway.

After parking behind the hardware store, she tucked the gun into her jeans and covered it with the shirt and jacket she'd put on earlier that morning. Taking a breath, she climbed out and entered the hardware store at the back through the delivery entrance. In the dim light of the empty area, she did her best to pull it together. Butch wouldn't be excited to see her to begin with. If he sensed how desperate she was, she feared he would run.

He wasn't in the office at the back. She started through the store, keeping an eye out for him. She was almost to the front when an employee asked if she needed help.

"I'm looking for Butch," she said, surprised that her voice sounded almost normal.

"He's on vacation and not expected back for a couple of weeks," the young man said.

Vacation? "It's urgent that I contact him. When did he leave?"

"I believe he planned to leave today."

"Could you give me his address? Maybe I can catch him if he hasn't left yet."

The young employee hesitated.

"Please. It's urgent."

"Well, I suppose it will be all right." He rattled off the address, and Frankie raced back the way she'd come.

Butch lived in a small house on the north side of town that, like most of Bozeman, had been completely remodeled. She wondered when and how much money it had cost. She prayed that he hadn't left yet and that he had been too scared to dip into the money.

As she parked on the street and got out, she noticed that the house looked deserted. The garage door was closed and there was a newspaper lying on the front step, unread. Her heart dropped to her feet as she walked toward the house, wondering what to do next.

That was when she heard a noise inside the house. As she approached the garage, she glanced into one of the small windows high on the door. Butch Clark was hurriedly packing for what looked like more than a two-week vacation.

HANK WATCHED DARREL, seeing him become more anxious and irritated with each passing hour. It hadn't been a surprise when the man had broken his word immediately, sending Trent after Frankie.

"Stay back. Don't let her spot you tailing her," Darrel had ordered. "She takes you to the money, you know what to do."

He'd felt his heart drop, afraid he knew exactly what Trent would do. All he could hope was that Frankie was as good at her job as he knew her to be and would spot the tail or be able to deal with Trent if she had to.

Darrel began pacing again. His pacing the cabin floor had turned out to be a godsend. He'd paid little attention to Hank as if he'd forgotten about him. Les had lain down on the bed and quickly gone to sleep.

Meanwhile, Hank had been working on the duct tape Trent had used to bind his wrists behind him to the chair. He'd found a rough spot on the wood where a screw was sticking out. He could feel the tape weakening as he sawed through layer after layer. It was tedious, but he had time, he kept telling himself. He had to be free when Frankie returned.

His head ached, but if he had a concussion it wasn't a bad one. The dizziness had passed and he was feeling stronger by the moment.

When Darrel's cell phone rang, the man practically jumped out of his thin skin. Hank stopped what he was doing for a moment. He could hear the entire conversation at both ends since Trent was talking so loudly.

"What do you mean you lost her?" Darrel demanded.

"She was headed toward the north end of

town but then suddenly veered off on a street. I stayed back like you said but then she was headed toward Main Street and she was gone."

Darrel swore. "You say she was headed toward the north side of town?"

"Yeah. I don't know why she suddenly—"

"She spotted a tail," he snapped. "Go back to the north side of town, where she was originally headed. Drive the streets until you find her. *Find her.*"

"Okay, I'll try, but—"

"Either you find her or you'd better keep going and hope I never find *you.* That clear enough for you?"

"I'll find her. I won't give up until I do."

J.J. WAS GETTING sick of lying in the back of the moving pickup under the tarps. He wasn't sure how much more of this he could take. But he had to know what Frankie was up to.

When she'd stopped the pickup the first time, she'd gotten out. He'd waited for a few moments and then taken a peek. He'd watched her go into the back of a hardware store before quickly covering up again. What was this about? None of it made any sense. She'd left the cowboy and gone shopping? Was it possible Hank Savage had known the man he'd picked up in the road? If so, then…

She'd come back sooner than he'd anticipated, the pickup door opening, closing, the engine starting and the truck moving again. Maybe she'd had to pick up something. An ax? A shovel? He'd shuddered at the thought.

The truck didn't go far before he felt something change. Frankie had been driving at a normal pace when suddenly she took off, turning this way and that. He had to hang on now or be tossed around the back of the pickup like a rag doll. What was going on?

When she finally slowed down and quit turning, she seemed to be backtracking. He'd been listening to the sounds around him. They'd been in traffic but now it had grown quieter. She brought the pickup to a stop. He heard her exit the truck. He listened, afraid to take a peek yet. He definitely had the feeling that they were in a residential part of town. He could hear the sound of someone using a leaf blower some distance away.

When he couldn't take the suspense any longer, he carefully rose and pushed back the edge of the tarp aside to peer out. What he saw shocked him. Frankie had pulled a gun and was now about to open someone's garage door. But before she could, the door suddenly began to rise with the sound of the mechanical engine pulling it up.

He heard an engine start up in the garage and saw Frankie step in front of the idling car, the gun raised to windshield level. "Stop, Butch!"

The car engine revved. Whoever was behind the wheel had backed the vehicle into the garage. For a fast getaway? The fool either had a death wish or was playing his luck. Either way, J.J. could see that Frankie was in trouble. The driver didn't seem afraid of the gun she was holding.

He threw back the tarp and jumped down to run at her, shoving her out of the way as the car came screaming out of the garage. He had drawn his own gun, but when he saw that the fool behind the wheel wasn't going to stop, he threw himself onto the hood and crashed into the windshield.

The driver hit his brakes hard. J.J. groped for something to hang on to but, failing, slid to the concrete, coming down hard. As he started to get up, he heard the engine rev again. He saw Frankie had the passenger-side door open and was screaming for the man behind the wheel to get out of the car.

He rolled to the side, but not quick enough. The door had caught him in the back of the head and the lights went out.

the gun

Chapter Twenty-One

Butch rattled the handcuffs holding him re-
strained to the passenger-side door of his
car. "How do I know you aren't going to kill
me?" His voice squeaked—just as it had when
she'd jumped into the car as he was trying
to get away. She'd shoved the barrel of the
gun into the side of his head and told him she
was going to kill him if he didn't stop. He'd
stopped.

"You don't." She'd grabbed the keys and
forced him at gunpoint into the passenger seat
to handcuff him to the door.

"Who was that back there?" Butch asked
now as they drove away from his house.

"A cop." She glanced in the rearview mirror over the top of all Butch's belongings
he'd loaded. So far no tail. Also no J.J. She'd
checked for a pulse. He had still been breathing but wasn't conscious. She'd taken his cop
gun. At least now she had real bullets and a

vehicle that whoever Darrel had sent to follow her wouldn't know. Her tail would find the pickup at the house—if he found the house at all.

"*A cop?* You said you wouldn't go to the cops."

Frankie shook her head, keeping her attention on her driving. "I wanted to keep you out of it, Butch. Unfortunately, I had no idea just how deep you really were in all this. You lied to me, but for your sake and mine, you'd better not be lying to me now."

"I'm not." He sounded whiny. She could see why Naomi had dumped him. But he must have been the closest thing she had to a friend she could confide in.

"Why didn't you tell Naomi to give the money back right away?" she asked.

"I did. She wouldn't listen. She really thought she could get away with it."

Frankie shot him a look. "Kind of like you."

"Hey, what could I have done? They didn't know about me. I didn't know them. Naomi was dead. I knew where the money was hidden. So I waited to see what happened. Nothing happened. Until you showed up."

"You could have gone to the cops," she snapped. And then none of this would be happening. Hank wouldn't be in serious trouble back at the cabin and she wouldn't be racing out of town with two guns, one actually loaded, with a man handcuffed to the car and only a hope and a prayer that he wasn't lying to her.

She glanced over at Butch. He looked scared. That, she decided, was good. "I have to ask. Why did you wait to get the money?"

He turned to look out his side window. They'd passed Gallatin Gateway and were almost to Big Sky and Cardwell Ranch, where he swore Naomi had buried the money. "I had this crazy idea that they were watching the place where she buried it, you know, just waiting for me to show up so they could kill me like they did her."

Frankie thought about telling him what Darrel had said about Naomi's death. That was if he was telling the truth. Either way, Butch might have been able to save her—if he'd gone to the cops right away.

Nor did she point out that there was little chance Darrel would be watching the ranch 24/7 even if he knew where the money was buried.

She turned onto the dirt road into the ranch, her mind racing. What would she do when she found the money? Hank had been right. She couldn't trust Darrel to keep his word. He said she wouldn't be followed. A lie. Once she handed over the money...

As she drove into the ranch yard, Butch pointed in the direction of a stand of trees. The land dropped to a small creek. Frankie groaned inwardly. She just hoped that Naomi was smart enough to bury the money where the rising water didn't send it into the Gallatin River. It could be in the Gulf of Mexico by now otherwise.

"Tell me exactly where it is," she said as she brought the car to a stop at the edge of the incline to the creek.

"There's a statue or something, she said, near the water."

Frankie frowned. "A statue?" she asked as she looked down the hill and saw pine trees and a babbling brook but no statue.

"Maybe not a statue, but—"

"A birdbath," she said, spotting it in a stand of trees. She quickly put the keys in her pocket, opened the door and, grabbing the shovel she'd taken from his garage, got out. As she did, she glanced toward the house and saw no one. Maybe she would get lucky. She needed some luck right now.

It was a short walk down to a stand of trees on a rise above the creek. Someone had put a birdbath down here. Near it were two benches as if someone in the family came down here to watch the birds beside the river. Dana? She couldn't see the marshal sitting here patiently.

The birdbath, apparently made of solid concrete, proved to be heavier than it looked. She could have used Butch, but she didn't trust the man. She tried dislodging it and inching it over out of the way, wasting valuable minutes.

Finally, she just knocked it over, which took all her strength as it was. Then she began to dig. She wondered how Naomi had managed moving the birdbath and realized it had probably been her idea, the benches and the birdbath—after she'd buried the rest of the money.

The bag wasn't buried deep. Frankie pulled it out, sweating with the effort and the constant fear of what might be happening back at the cabin. The bag looked like one used by banks. It was large and heavy. She opened it just enough to see that it was stuffed with money, lots of money in large bills, and quickly closed it.

Leaving the shovel, she climbed back up the incline. As she topped it, she saw Dana standing by the side of the car.

WHEN J.J. CAME TO, he was lying on the grass with a monstrous headache. His gun was gone.

So was Frankie and the car and its driver. All she'd left behind was the cowboy's pickup.

J.J. limped into the house through the open garage door. The house felt deserted. He was moving painfully through the living room when he thought he heard a car door slam. Was it possible Frankie had come back? He couldn't believe she'd left him passed out on the concrete and hadn't even called an ambulance. But she'd managed to take his gun.

He pressed himself against a wall out of sight of the hallway as he heard footfalls in the garage. One person moving slowly, no doubt looking for him. Why had Frankie come back now? It didn't matter. He was ready for her.

He smiled to himself as he waited to pounce. She wouldn't know what hit her.

As a figure came around the corner, he lunged. He didn't realize his mistake until it was too late. The figure spun as if sensing him coming and caught him square in the face with his fist. As he took the blow, he realized that the figure was way too large to be Frankie, way too powerful and way too male.

"Who the hell are you?" he heard the man say as he crashed on the floor at the man's feet. Before he could answer, he heard the man pump a bullet into his gun. He rolled over, struggling to pull out his badge, when he heard the first shot echo through the room. The burn of the bullet searing through his flesh came an instant later.

He tried to get up, tried to get his badge out. The second shot hit him in the chest and knocked him back to the floor. As the big man moved closer, J.J. saw that it was the tough guy who'd searched the pickup earlier at the cabin.

"You've really screwed up now," J.J. managed to say as he felt his life's blood seeping from him. "You just killed a cop."

"I'D LIKE TO tell you that this isn't what it looks like," Frankie said as she approached Dana. She saw that the woman had her cell phone clutched in her hand and knew at once that she'd already called the marshal.

"I thought you and Hank had gone back to Idaho," Dana said. Her voice trembled as her gaze took in the weapon Frankie had stuck in the waist of her jeans. Her shirt and jacket had come up during her battle with the birdbath.

"How long before Hud gets here?" Frankie asked.

"Where's Hank?" the older woman asked. She sounded as scared as Frankie felt.

"He's in trouble. I need to get back to him, Dana. I'm a private investigator. It's too long a story to get into right now. I need to leave before Hud gets here."

Dana shook her head, tears in her eyes. "I knew something was wrong. But I hoped…" Inside the car, Butch began to yell for Dana to help him. "That man is handcuffed and you have a…gun."

Frankie knew she couldn't stand here arguing. She started past Dana when she heard the sound of a siren. Moments later she saw the flashing lights as the SUV topped a rise and came blaring into the ranch yard.

She let out a shaky breath and felt tears burn her eyes. There was still time before sundown. But that would mean talking her way out of this, and right now, covered in mud, holding a bag of even dirtier drug money, she wasn't sure she had the words. All she knew was that she had to convince the marshal before sundown.

HUD SHUT OFF the siren. As he climbed out, he took in the scene. The man handcuffed in the car tried to slide down out of sight. Dana stepped to Hud, and he put his arm around her before he turned his attention to the young woman his son had fallen in love with. "Frankie?"

She held out the bag. "It's the drug money.

They have Hank. If I don't give the money to them by sundown…" Her voice broke.

He nodded and stepped to her to take the money. "And that?" he asked, tilting his head toward the man in the car.

"It's Butch Clark, Naomi's old boyfriend. He's known where the money was buried all these years."

Hud nodded and glanced at his watch. "We have a little time. Whatever's happened, we will deal with it. You say they have Hank." She nodded. "Tell me everything," he said as he walked her toward the house.

"What about him?" Dana asked behind them.

"He's fine where he is for the time being," Hud said without a backward glance. Inside the house, Frankie quickly cleaned up at the kitchen sink as she told him about the man stumbling out onto the highway, being taken to the cabin, the demand for the money and Hank being injured.

Dana gasped at that point, her eyes filling with tears, but she held it together. Hud had to hand it to her—she was a strong woman and always had been. Her son was injured and being held by drug dealers. It scared the hell out of him, but Dana fortunately wasn't one to panic in a crisis. He appreciated that right now.

"Okay," he said when Frankie finished. "You say Darrel gave you an unloaded gun." He picked up the Glock he'd taken from her. "This one is loaded."

She nodded. "J.J. must have followed us. He was hiding in the back of the pickup. He tried to stop Butch when Butch was attempting to flee. He was hit by the car, but he was alive the last time I saw him."

Hud studied the woman, amazed by her resilience as well as her bravery. "You don't think Darrel will let the two of you go when you take him the money, right?"

She shook her head. "He doesn't want to kill us, but…"

"What will you do?" Dana asked her husband.

"The first thing is read Butch Clark his rights and get him locked up in my jail so he's not a problem." Hud pulled out his phone and called a deputy to come handle it. As he hung up, he looked at Frankie. "I need to take you back to Hank's pickup. There's time before sundown. Then you drive back to the cabin with the bag of money."

"Where will you be?" Dana asked.

"In the back of the pickup. I'll need to grab

a few things and have Bozeman backup standing by." He got to his feet. "Let's go get Hank."

HANK WATCHED DARREL pace the cabin floor and worked surreptitiously at the thick tape binding his wrists behind him to the chair. He'd made a point of acting like he was still dizzy and weak from the blow, mumbling to himself incoherently until Darrel had removed the duct tape.

"Water," Hank had mouthed. "Please."

Darrel had gotten him some, holding it to his lips so he could take a few gulps. "She'll be back," Hank said when he took the water away. "With the money." And that was the part that terrified him the most, because he had no doubt that his former classmate would go back on his word. No way were he and Frankie walking out of here alive. "She does what she says she's going to do."

Darrel had started pacing again. Hank saw him looking out the window where the sun was dropping toward the horizon at a pace that had them both worried. Now the man turned to look at him and laughed. "You sure about that? If I were her, I'd take the money and go as far away from here as I possibly could."

"That's you. Frankie isn't like that." But right now, he wished she was. At least she would be safe. He'd gotten her into this. He deserved what he got. But Frankie... He couldn't bear to think of her being hurt, let alone—

"You'd better be right." Darrel sounded sad, as if he would be sorry for killing him. "I hate the way this whole thing spiraled out of control, and all because of that girlfriend of yours."

Hank couldn't argue with that. "I fell in love with a woman I didn't know. She hid so much from me, including stealing your money."

"And you think you know this one?" Darrel scoffed at that. "All women are alike. You really haven't learned anything since high school, have you. They will double-cross you every time. I knew this one—" He stopped talking to turn and look out the window again. He'd heard what Hank had.

The sound of his pickup's engine could be heard as the truck approached the cabin. Frankie had come back with the money. And before sundown.

"I've got to hand it to you, Hank. This woman really is something. If she's got the money, then I'd say this one is a keeper."

"Keep your promise. Let us go. We want nothing to do with any of this and you know it."

"Yeah, I hear you," Darrel said, actually

sounding as if he regretted what was going to happen next. "We're going to have to talk about that." He stepped over to the bed and kicked the end of it. Les stirred from a deep sleep. "Wake up. We've got company. Go out and make sure she's alone."

"Me? Why do I have to—"

Darrel cuffed the man on the head. "Go!"

Les stumbled from the bed, clearly still half-asleep, and headed for the door. Darrel stood at the window, his back to him. Hank worked feverishly at the tape. Just a little more. He felt it give.

FRANKIE DID AS Hud had told her and parked next to the panel van, out of sight of the cabin. She stayed in the pickup, sitting behind the wheel, after she'd turned off the engine, waiting.

She desperately wanted to see Hank. She had to know that he was all right. But the marshal had assured her—Hank was safer if they did things his way.

She wasn't going to argue. She was thankful that she wasn't facing this completely alone. Because she had a bad feeling that once she got out of the pickup with the money, both she and Hank were as good as dead.

Les frowned as he saw where she was parking. He walked around the front of the vehicles to stop in front of the pickup. "Get out!" he ordered, still frowning. He looked as if he'd just woken up, which made her heart race. What had Darrel done with Hank after she'd left that he'd let Les sleep?

When she didn't get out, he stepped up to try the door and, finding it locked, glanced back at the cabin before he began to fumble for his gun. That was when Hud rose and cold-cocked him with the butt end of a shotgun. The man dropped between the pickup and panel van without a sound.

As the marshal hopped down out of sight of the cabin windows, Frankie opened her door.

"Leave the bag with the money here," Hud said as he cuffed and gagged Les before rolling his body under the pickup. "Go into the cabin to check on Hank. When Darrel asks, tell him that Les took it from you. I need to know how many men are in there."

She nodded and whispered, "Trent was following me. I don't see his vehicle, so I don't think he's back yet. It should just be Darrel."

"Let's hope," Hud said and motioned for her to go before Darrel got suspicious.

Frankie headed for the cabin, praying with each step that Hank was all right. As she pushed open the door, the first thing she saw was Darrel. He had a gun in his hand, pointed at her heart. Her gaze leaped past him to Hank. She saw pleasure flash in his blue eyes at seeing her, then concern. He was still in the chair, but he seemed to feel better than the last time she'd seen him.

"Where's my money?" Darrel demanded, already sounding furious as if he'd worked himself up in the time she'd been gone. The door was open behind her, but he was blocking her from going to Hank.

"Les has it. He took it from me." She could see that he didn't believe her. She described the bag. "I didn't touch the money, but the bag is heavy, and when I looked inside… I think all but the five grand she used for a down payment on the house is in there. Or at least enough to get you out of hot water. Now let us go."

Darrel shook his head, still blocking her from going to Hank, and yelled, "Les!" Not hearing an answer, he yelled again. "Bring the money in here."

She looked past him and saw Hank slowly pull his wrists free from behind him. He shook them out as if he'd lost all feeling in his arms after all this time of being taped to the chair. She gave a small shake of her head for him not to move.

"Les is probably out there counting the money," Frankie said, hoping the man would step outside, where the marshal was waiting. "Or has already taken off with the bag."

"On foot?" Darrel demanded and grabbed her as they both heard the scrape of chair legs on the floor.

HANK MOVED QUICKLY. Darrel was right about one thing. He'd always been better at sports than his classmate. Fortunately, that athletic prowess benefited him now when he needed it the most.

As Darrel turned, there was a moment of surprise, a hesitation that cost him. He was about to put the barrel of the gun to Frankie's head when Hank hit him in the side of his head with his fist and grabbed the gun. Darrel staggered from the blow but didn't go down. His grip on Frankie seemed to be the only thing holding him up.

Hank twisted the gun from the man's hand. The two grappled with it for a moment before Darrel let out a cry of pain. Frankie shoved him off her and pulled the Glock from behind her to point it at the drug dealer as he went down. She looked over at Hank, who stood beside her, the gun in his hand pointed at Darrel's heart as well.

Behind them Frankie heard the marshal say, "Well, look at the two of you. It appears you didn't even need my help." There was a smile in his voice as well as relief as he reached for his phone to let the cops know that he'd take that backup now. "I have two perps who need to be taken to jail. Also going to need a medic as well," he said, looking at the dried blood on his son's temple. "And I'm going to need a ride back to Big Sky."

"We could have given you a ride," Hank said after his father cuffed Darrel and read him his rights. Frankie could hear sirens in the distance. She leaned against Hank, his arm around her. She told herself that all she needed was a hot shower and she'd stop shaking.

"I thought you two might like some time together. But I guess you know this means you can't leave for Idaho for a while," the marshal said.

Hank glanced at her. "I think we're good with that."

FRANKIE HELPED HERSELF to another stack of silver-dollar-sized pancakes, slathered on butter and then drowned them in chokecherry syrup. She couldn't remember ever being this hungry.

So much had happened and in such a short

time. She would have worried about that before Hank. She was no longer worried about it happening too fast. Instead, she was ready for the future in a way she'd never been before. She felt free, everything looking brighter, even before she'd heard the news about J.J.

Trent had been arrested and confessed everything, including killing the cop. He'd said it was self-defense, that J.J. had been reaching for his gun. But the Glock hadn't been found on the cop—or at the scene—because Frankie had taken it.

After hearing what all the cops had against him, including assaulting Hank and dealing drugs, along with killing an unarmed cop, Trent decided to make a deal for a lesser sentence for what he knew about the drug ring and Darrel's part in it.

Frankie could feel Dana watching her eat and smiling. "So you're a private investigator," she said. "Sounds dangerous. I was thinking that if you were to get married and have babies…"

Swallowing the bite in her mouth, Frankie grinned at her. "Hank hasn't asked me to marry him and you're talking babies."

"He'll ask. I've never seen my son happier."

Frankie thought about the hot shower she'd stepped into last night after they'd returned to their cabin. Hank had joined her, sans his clothes this time. Their lovemaking had been so passionate under the warm spray that she felt her cheeks heat at the memory even now.

"He makes me happy too," she said and took another bite of pancake.

"I can tell," Dana said with a secret smile. "You're glowing this morning. If it wasn't too early, I'd think you were pregnant."

Frankie almost choked on her bite of pancake. True, last night in the shower they hadn't used protection, but pregnant? She swallowed.

"Would that be so awful?" Dana asked.

She thought about it for one whole instant and smiled. "Not at all." The thought of her child growing up on this ranch made her happy. She and Hank had talked about the future last night after their shower. He'd asked how she'd feel about living on the ranch, if she would still want to work as a private investigator, if she wanted children, how she felt about dogs and cats and horses.

She'd laughed as she'd listened to his questions and grinned. "I'd love living on this ranch, I'd probably want to be involved in ranching with you rather than continue working as an investigator, I do want children, and I love dogs, cats and horses. After that horseback ride with you, I'm hooked."

"Was it the horseback ride or me that got you hooked?" he'd asked with a grin.

"By the way, where *is* my son?" Dana asked, interrupting her thoughts.

Frankie helped herself to a slice of ham and just a couple more pancakes. "He went to say goodbye to Naomi."

HANK PARKED IN the pines beside the Gallatin River as he'd done so many times before. This time he was anxious to reach the water. He climbed out and wound his way through the tall pines. A breeze swayed the tops of the boughs, whispering. The sound of the river grew louder. He could feel the sun as it fingered its way through the pines. He breathed in the scent of pine and water as if smelling it for the first time.

Ahead, he got his first glimpse of the cliff. It was dark and ominous-looking, shadowed this morning until the sun rose high enough to turn it a golden hue.

It seemed strange to make this trek after everything that had happened. He wasn't sure he could ever forgive Naomi for what she did. He and Frankie had almost gotten killed because of a bag full of money. He still couldn't believe that she'd died protecting it.

He broke out of the pines and stood for a

moment at the edge of the trees. The breeze was stronger here. It rippled the moving surface of the river and ruffled his hair at his neck. He took off his Stetson and turned his face up to the breeze, letting it do what it would with his normally tousled dark hair. He couldn't help but think of Frankie's fingers in the wet strands last night as she pulled him down to her mouth. The memory of the two of them laughing and making love in the shower made him smile for a moment before he dropped down to the edge of the river.

He listened to the gentle roar of the water as it rushed over the rocks and pooled at his feet. The breeze lifted his hair as he looked up. The ledge was a dark line cut across the rock surface. For three years it had lured him back here, looking for answers. Now he knew it all.

He thought of Naomi standing on that ledge that night with Tamara. He'd always thought of her as helpless, defenseless, fragile and delicate. He'd always felt he had to protect her— even her memory. He could almost see her teetering on that ledge. Would they have let her live if she'd given them the money? They would never know. But he knew now that she was willing to die rather than give it up.

Hank hated what that said about her. He thought of her mother working all those years to support herself and her daughter. Was that what had made Naomi think she had to steal? Or was it a sickness that had started with shoplifting and had gotten away from her?

Naomi's mother had made a life for herself with a man who loved her. Lillian would survive this since he suspected she knew her daughter much better than he ever had.

He waited to feel Naomi's spirit, to see a ghostly flash of her. He expected to feel her presence as he had so many times before. He'd always thought she was waiting here for him, pleading with him to find her killer.

Now he felt nothing but the summer breeze coming off the cool surface of the river. He stared at the ledge through the sunlight, but felt nothing. Naomi was gone—if she'd ever really been here.

As he settled his Stetson back on his head, he realized it was true. Naomi's ghost had been banished for good. He felt lighter. Freer. The cliff no longer held him prisoner. Neither did Naomi.

"Goodbye," he said, glancing once more at the cliff before he started back to the pickup. He realized that he could walk away without ever looking back, without ever coming back. It felt good. *He* felt good. He couldn't wait to get to Frankie. They were leaving today, but they would return.

He drove toward the ranch, excited about life for the first time in three years. He couldn't wait to see Frankie. But first there was something he had to do.

HUD LOOKED UP to find his son standing in the doorway of his office. "Is everything all right?" he asked, immediately concerned. Hank had an odd look on his face.

"I need to ask a favor."

He and Hank hadn't talked much since everything had happened. His son's statement about what had transpired at the cabin had filled in a lot of the blanks. He'd wondered how Hank had taken the news about Naomi and if he would finally be able to put the past behind him—with Frankie's help.

"Name it. If there's something I can do…"

Hank came into his office and closed the door behind him. His son seemed nervous. That, he realized, was what he'd been picking up on the moment he saw him standing in the doorway. He'd never seen him nervous. Angry, yes. But not like this. He realized that whatever his son had to ask him, it was serious.

"When I asked you for Grandmother's ring—"

Hud swore. He'd forgotten the day that his

son had come to him and asked for his grandmother's ring. Since he was a little boy, Hank had been told that his grandmother Cardwell's ring would go to Mary, but that his grandmother Savage's ring was his for the day that he met the love of his life and asked her to marry him.

But when Hank had asked for it, saying he was going to marry Naomi no matter what anyone thought because they were all wrong about her, Hud had turned him down.

"I'm sorry, son. I can't let you give Naomi the ring." He and Dana had discussed it numerous times in the days before Hank had come to him. They'd seen that Naomi was pushing marriage and could tell that their son wasn't ready. Add to that Naomi's...problems, as Dana referred to them.

"She's a thief," Hud had said. "Not just that. You know she's pressing Hank to leave the ranch to work for her stepfather."

"Maybe it's what he wants."

Hud remembered being so angry with his wife that he'd gotten out of bed and pulled on his jeans, had left. He and Dana seldom argued. But that night he hadn't been able to take any more. He'd driven up to Hebgen Lake to see his father, Brick, an old-time lawman. Hud had named one of his twin son's after his father; the other one after Dana's father, Angus.

He and his father had often been at odds, and yet that night, the old lawman was who he'd gone to for help. It was the same year that Brick had passed away. He remembered waking him up that night. Why he chose his father was a mystery since the two of them had spent years at odds.

But Brick had given him good advice. "Stick to your guns. He's your son. You know him. He won't love you for it. Quite the contrary." He'd seen the gleam in his old man's eyes and known that he was talking about the two of them and the years they'd spent knocking heads. "You're doing him a real disservice if you just give in to keep the peace."

He'd stayed the night, driven back the next morning and told Dana that he wasn't giving Hank the ring if he asked for it again. She'd been furious with him, but he'd stuck to his guns, even though it had cost him dearly both with his wife and his son. He'd never known if Hank would have married Naomi anyway if she'd lived.

"When you'd asked for my mother's ring, I thought you were making a mistake," Hud said now. "I didn't want you giving the ring to the wrong woman and later regretting it when you met the love of your life."

Hank shook his head. "It was your decision since my grandmother apparently put you in charge of it."

"Actually, it was your grandpa Brick," he said.

"Did he also advise you to not give it to me?" Hank asked.

Hud wanted to be as honest with him as possible. "Your mother and I argued about it. I had to leave, so I drove up to your grandfather's place and asked him what I should do."

Hank's eyes widened. "You actually asked your father for advice?"

"It happens," Hud said and smiled. "Admittedly, it took years before I found myself doing that."

With a grin, his son said, "It's hard for me to admit that you were right."

"I understand."

"But I'm back. I want to give Grandmother's ring to Frankie, and I'm not taking no for an answer this time. Rightfully, it's my ring to do—"

"I totally agree." Hud reached into the drawer where he'd put the ring after meeting Frankie.

"You have it here?"

"I had a feeling you'd want it," he said.

Hank shook his head as he took the small velvet box. "I will never understand you."

"Probably not." He watched his son lift the tiny lid and saw Hank's eyes light up as he stared down at the diamond engagement ring.

"Do you think she'll like it?" The nervousness was back.

"She'll love it because she loves you."

FALL WAS IN the air that late day in August. The seasons changed at will in Montana and even more so in the canyon so close to the mountains. One day would feel like summer, the next fall, and in the blink of an eye snow would begin.

Dried leaves rustled on the aspens as Frankie rode her horse out of the pines and into the wide meadow. She breathed in the crisp, clean air, reined in her horse and dismounted at the edge of the mountain to wait for Hank. He'd been acting strange all day. She knew it had to be because they would be leaving here—at least temporarily.

Last night they'd lain in bed, wrapped up in each other after making love, and talked about the future.

"Are you sure you'd be happy at the ranch? Because if not, we could—"

She'd kissed him to stop the words. "Hank, I love the ranch. I can't imagine living anywhere more…magical."

He'd eyed her suspiciously. "You aren't just saying that because you're crazy in love with me."

"I am crazy in love with you, but no, I wouldn't lie to you." He'd told her that the ghost of Naomi was gone, but she wondered. He still thought that because Naomi could never be happy at the ranch, neither could any other woman. She knew it would take time for him to realize that she was nothing like Naomi.

"Look at your mother, Hank. She loves this ranch just like her mother did. Isn't that why your grandmother left it to her, passing on the legacy? And all the women your uncles are married to. They're all happy living here," she continued. "Isn't it possible I'm more like your mother than…?" She wouldn't say "Naomi." "Than some other woman might be?"

He'd nodded and smiled as he kissed her. "I feel so lucky. I keep wanting to pinch myself. I guess that's why it's so hard for me to believe this is real. I never dreamed…" He kissed her again. "That I could be this happy."

Now, as he rode up beside her, his Stetson hiding much of his handsome face, she felt almost afraid. He'd been so quiet all morning and it wasn't like him to hang back on his horse the way he had. As she watched him slowly ride toward her, her heart fluttered. She was crazy in love with this man, just as she had told him. And yet maybe this was too fast for both of them.

She thought of J.J. and quickly pushed it away. Hank wasn't J.J. Whatever was going on with Hank—

At a sound in the pines, she looked past Hank to see Hud and Dana come riding out of the trees. Behind them were Mary and Chase, and behind them were Stacy and the rest of the family.

Frankie blinked. "What?"

Hank looked up and grinned. "I am terrible at keeping secrets, and this one was killing me this morning," he said as he dismounted and took her in his arms. "I hope you don't mind."

Mind that he'd invited his entire family on their horseback ride? She felt confused, and yet as everyone rode toward them, they were all smiling. One of the uncles brought up the rear with a huge bunch of helium balloons.

"Hank?" she asked. He only hugged her tightly. She could see the emotion in his face and felt her heart take off like a wild horse in a thunderstorm. "Hank?" she repeated as they all began to dismount. His uncle was handing out the balloons. "I think you'd better tell me what's going on."

The family had formed a circle around them and seemed to be waiting, just like Frankie. Hank turned to her, taking both of her hands in his.

"I know this is fast, but if I've learned anything, it's that when things are right, they're right," Hank said and cleared his voice. "You are the most amazing woman I've ever met. You're smart, talented, independent to a fault, stubborn as the day is long, courageous—way too courageous, I might add—determined and…beautiful and loving and everything I could want in one unique woman."

She tried to swallow around the lump in her throat. "Thank you, I think."

A murmur of laughter rose from the group gathered.

"You saved my life in so many ways," Hank continued. "I can never thank you enough for that. And you've brought just joy to my life when I never thought I'd ever feel again. Frankie…" He seemed at a loss for words.

"Come on. Get on with it," someone yelled at the back of the group, followed by another burst of laughter.

Hank laughed with them. "They all know

that I'm like my father, a man of few words."
Yet another burst of laughter. "But if I forget
to tell you all of these things in the future, I
wanted to be sure and say them today. I love
you, Francesca 'Frankie' Brewster, with all
my heart."

She watched him drop to one knee to the
applause of the group.

He looked up at her, his blue eyes filled
with love. She felt her own eyes fill with tears
as he asked, "Will you do me the honor of
marrying me?"

The tears overflowed and cascaded down
her cheeks as she nodded, overwhelmed by
all of this.

He reached into his pocket and pulled out
a small velvet box. "This ring was my grandmother Savage's." He took it out, held her left
hand and slipped it on her finger.

She gazed down at it. "It's beautiful," she
said as he got to his feet. Looking into his
handsome face, she whispered, "I love you,"
and threw her arms around him.

As the two of them turned, his family let
out a cheer and released the balloons. Frankie
looked up toward the heavens as dozens of
colorful balloons took flight up into Montana's big sky. She'd never seen a more beautiful sight because of what they all represented.

Hank hugged her and then everyone else was hugging her, the meadow full of love and congratulations. "This is only the beginning," he said with a laugh. "You always wanted a big family. Well, you're going to have one now."

"I never dreamed..." she said and couldn't finish. How could she have dreamed that one day she'd meet a cowboy and he'd take her home and give her a family?

* * * * *

Cardwell Ranch: Montana Legacy
continues in 2020
with a brand-new trilogy!

Until then, look for more great books from
New York Times *bestselling author*
B.J. Daniels.

Here's a peek at Just His Luck,
from the Sterling's Montana series.

Chapter One

Another scream rose in her throat as the icy water rushed in around her. She fought to free herself, but the ropes that bound her wrists to the steering wheel held tight, chafing her skin until it tore and bled. Her throat was raw from screaming while outside the car the wind kicked up whitecaps on the pond. The waves sloshed against the windows. Inside the car, water rose around her feet before climbing up her legs to lap at her waist.

She pleaded for help as the water began to rise up her chest. As it touched her throat, she screamed even though she knew there wasn't anyone out there who would be coming to her rescue. Certainly not the person standing on the shore watching.

The pond was outside of town, away from everything. She knew now that was why her killer had chosen it. Worse, no one would be looking for her after all the bridges she'd burned tonight at her high school graduation party.

"You're big on torturing people," her killer had said. "Not so much fun when the shoe is on the other foot, huh."

More than half-drunk, the bitter taste of betrayal in her mouth, she'd wanted to beg for her life. But her pride wouldn't have let her—even if the drug coursing through her veins would have. As her hands were bound to the steering wheel, she was sure that the only reason this was happening was to scare her. But she thought this had gone far enough. No one would actually kill her. Not even someone she'd bullied at school.

She was Ariel Matheson. Everyone wanted to be her friend. Everyone wanted to be her, the sexy, spoiled rich girl. No one hated her enough to go through with this. Even when the car had been pushed into the pond, she'd told herself that her new baby-blue SUV wouldn't sink. Or if it did, the water wouldn't be deep enough that she'd drown.

The dank water splashed into her face. Frantic, she tried to sit up higher, but the seat belt and the rope on her wrists held her down. The car lurched under her as it wallowed half-full of water on the rough surface of the pond. Waves splashed over the windshield, obscuring the lights of Whitefish, Montana, as the SUV slowly sank and she felt the last few minutes of her life slipping away.

She spit out a mouthful of water and told herself that this wasn't happening. Things like this didn't happen to her. This was not the way her life would end. It couldn't be.

Panic made her suck in another mouthful of awful-tasting water. She tried to hold her breath as she told herself that she was destined for so much more. The Girl Most Likely to End Up with Everything She Wanted, it said in her yearbook.

Bubbles rose around her as the car filled to the headliner, forcing her to let out the breath she'd been holding. This was real. This wasn't just to scare her.

The last thing she saw before the SUV sank the rest of the way was her killer standing on the bank in the dark night, watching her die. Would anyone miss her? Mourn her? She'd made so many enemies. Would anyone even come looking for her in the days ahead? Her parents would think that she'd run away. Her friends…

Fury replaced her fear. They thought she was a bitch before? As water filled her lungs, she swore revenge. If she could do it over? She'd make them pay.

*Available September 2019 wherever
HQN Books are sold.*